MONTANA MAVERICKS

Welcome to Big Sky Country, home of the Montana Mavericks! Where free-spirited men and women discover love on the range...

BROTHERS AND BRONCOS

Romance is in the air for the ranchers of Bronco, but someone is watching from the sidelines. A man from the town's past could be behind the mysterious messages, but does he pose a threat to Bronco's future? With their happily-ever-afters at stake, the bighearted cowboys will do what it takes to protect their beloved town— and the women they can't live without!

IN THE RING WITH THE MAVERICK

Cowgirl Audrey Hawkins has fought for years to succeed as a woman in the rodeo world. Now that she and her sisters have landed in Bronco, she's determined to make a name for herself— even if it means pitting herself against Jack Burris, one of the best riders on the circuit. Jack is too cocky, too handsome... and, unfortunately, *really* hard to resist!

Dear Reader,

I am so happy to be back in Bronco, Montana. I've grown fond of the people I've met there, and I'm thrilled to be able to tell their stories.

This month, I'm bringing you the romance between Jack Burris and Audrey Hawkins. Jack is the younger brother of rodeo superstar Geoff Burris, the hero of *A Kiss at the Mistletoe Rodeo*. Jack is doing his best to step out of his brother's shadow and make a name for himself. Audrey is a third-generation rodeo queen who performs alongside her three sisters.

Audrey and Jack are very driven people. They have professional goals and won't let anything get in the way—not even falling in love. When they're pitted against each other in a battle of the sexes event, they decide a romance between them is out of the question. But fate has a way of stepping in and changing even the best-laid plans.

I hope you enjoy *In the Ring with the Maverick* as much as I enjoyed writing it!

I love hearing from my readers. Feel free to stop by my website, kathydouglassbooks.com, and leave me a message. While you're there, sign up for my monthly newsletter so you can be the first to see my new covers, enter giveaways and get previews of my upcoming books. You can also find me on Facebook, Instagram, BookBub and Twitter.

Thank you for your support.

Happy reading!

Kathy

In the Ring with the Maverick

KATHY DOUGLASS

HARLEQUIN

**SPECIAL
EDITION**

If you purchased this book without a cover you should be aware
that this book is stolen property. It was reported as "unsold and
destroyed" to the publisher, and neither the author nor the
publisher has received any payment for this "stripped book."

Special thanks and acknowledgment are given to
Kathy Douglass for her contribution to
the Montana Mavericks: Brothers & Broncos miniseries.

Recycling programs
for this product may
not exist in your area.

ISBN-13: 978-1-335-72408-3

In the Ring with the Maverick

Copyright © 2022 by Harlequin Enterprises ULC

All rights reserved. No part of this book may be used or reproduced in
any manner whatsoever without written permission except in the case of
brief quotations embodied in critical articles and reviews.

This is a work of fiction. Names, characters, places and incidents
are either the product of the author's imagination or are used fictitiously.
Any resemblance to actual persons, living or dead, businesses,
companies, events or locales is entirely coincidental.

For questions and comments about the quality of this book,
please contact us at CustomerService@Harlequin.com.

Harlequin Enterprises ULC
22 Adelaide St. West, 41st Floor
Toronto, Ontario M5H 4E3, Canada
www.Harlequin.com

Printed in U.S.A.

Kathy Douglass came by her love of reading naturally—both of her parents were readers. She would finish one book and pick up another. Then she attended law school and traded romances for legal opinions.

After the birth of her two children, her love of reading turned into a love of writing. Kathy now spends her days writing the small-town contemporary novels she enjoys reading.

Books by Kathy Douglass

Harlequin Special Edition

Sweet Briar Sweethearts

The Single Mom's Second Chance
The Soldier Under Her Tree
Redemption on Rivers Ranch

The Fortunes of Texas: The Wedding Gift

A Fortune in the Family

Montana Mavericks: The Real Cowboys of Bronco Heights

In the Ring with the Maverick

Furever Yours

The City Girl's Homecoming

Montana Mavericks: What Happened to Beatrix?

The Maverick's Baby Arrangement

Visit the Author Profile page
at Harlequin.com for more titles.

This book is dedicated to Wayne Jordan.
You have supported me from the beginning,
my friend, and I appreciate you and all of the reviewers
at romanceincolor.com.

This book is also dedicated to my husband and sons.
I love you so much more than words can express.

Chapter One

"I can't believe how crowded it is in here," Jack Burris said to his younger brothers, Mike and Ross. He looked around Doug's, a hole-in-the-wall joint in Bronco, Montana. Doug's was located in the middle-class Valley section of town. With its scarred, mismatched tables, old jukebox and small dance floor, the bar wasn't the trendy type that the hoity-toity people who lived in the wealthier Bronco Heights section frequented. Tourists who came to Bronco, a town about two hours north of Billings, stepped right on by, if they could even find the place, but the tavern had a devoted clientele of locals.

But perhaps Doug Moore, the eightysomething-year-old proprietor, was trying to upgrade his establishment and attract a higher class of patron. Why else would he be open on a Sunday morning for brunch? Judging from the number of people currently enjoying the waffles, pancakes, grits, sausage, biscuits and gravy, Doug might have hit on something. Even so, Jack hoped the place didn't change too much. He liked hanging out here in the comfortable joint with his brothers and catching up with old friends when he was in town.

"Me neither," Mike added before shoveling a forkful of scrambled eggs into his mouth. After swallowing, he continued. "I don't know when he started it or how long he intends to keep it up, but I'm all for it."

"Me, too," Ross added. "I'm all for anything that means I don't have to cook."

Jack and his brothers were successful rodeo riders and spent most of their time on the road. They were at home this month to participate in the inaugural Bronco Summer Family Rodeo. Their oldest brother, Geoff, was one of the biggest stars in the sport and had been for the past several years. Unlike them, he hadn't come to town for the event. Instead, he was on a publicity tour, filming commercials and making guest appearances on talk shows to bring awareness of rodeo to a wider audience. His publicity tour was working, as evidenced by the number of rodeos that had been added to the schedule this year, including the one here in Bronco.

"And the food is delicious," Jack added, dragging the last bit of pancake around his plate and sopping up the remaining maple syrup before popping the bite into his mouth. He pushed his chair away from the table and stood. "I'm going for seconds."

"Bring me back some bacon," Ross said.

Mike waved his hand in the air signaling that he wanted more bacon, too.

"Got it," Jack said, striding across the crowded room. He joined a line near the buffet that was set up at the far end of the bar. While Jack waited, he heard the ring of feminine laughter. The joyous sound made him pause and he waited, hoping to hear it again. Odd. He'd heard women laugh countless times in his twenty-eight years and hadn't given it a second thought.

There was another burst of laughter and he spun around, determined to find the woman whose amusement he found so appealing. It took a moment, but he finally found the source of the bubbly sound. He took one look at the woman and his breath caught in his throat. She was positively beautiful. She had rich brown skin, shoulder-length black hair and brilliant brown eyes that sparkled with mischief. More than being simply gorgeous, she was radiant. There was a vibrancy about her that piqued Jack's interest and had him yearning to know her better.

Despite that intense longing, Jack forced himself to turn away. She was simply one woman. One of many that existed in the world. It made no sense to wax poetic about her just because she was beautiful and possessed an enchanting laugh. Enchanting? Since when did he use flowery words like that? He shook his head and stepped up to the bar, glancing from the empty serving trays to the woman behind the buffet.

"One minute and I'll be back with fresh bacon and flapjacks," she said before she lifted a metal tray and walked away.

"Sure," he replied, but she was already gone and he was talking to empty air.

"Sure what?"

Jack turned at the sound of the amused feminine voice. Before he'd laid eyes on the woman who'd spoken, he knew he was about to come face-to-face with the owner of that happy laugh.

"I was talking to the server," he said.

She looked at the empty spot and then back at him, a mischievous smile on her face. "Ah. The invisible server. I had an invisible friend when I was a kid," she said. She lowered her voice and leaned closer to him, as if she was about to confide a great secret, and he found himself leaning closer as well. She was petite, considerably shorter than his own six feet, and he had to bend so that she could whisper in his ear. "I shouldn't actually call her a friend since I wasn't really kind to her. She was more of a scapegoat, if truth be told. Whenever I did something that I shouldn't and my mother found out, I would blame it on Alex."

"The invisible friend," he said, smiling in return. He straightened and she did as well.

She nodded, her eyes dancing.

"And was your mother fooled?"

"Nah. She was much too smart. But she played along for a while. Then one day, after Alex had done something especially bad—I don't recall what it was—my mother told me that she wanted to meet Alex's mother to let her know how out of control her child was. Until they talked, Alex wasn't welcome in our home, and she forbid me to play with her."

"Wow. That's some good thinking."

"Yeah. And since I knew better than to bring someone into the house after I was expressly told not to, I had two choices. I could either get in trouble for my behavior or for hanging out with Alex. Sadly, Alex vanished from my life."

"Please tell me she didn't meet a disastrous end. That would be just too traumatic."

She laughed. "Don't worry, cowboy, there was

no bloody ending for her. She simply moved to another neighborhood, where I imagine she became the scapegoat for another seven-year-old girl."

Her laughter was infectious and he laughed with her and then leaned against the bar. "I could have used an invisible friend growing up. It would have saved me a lot of time spent on punishment. Of course, I had three brothers to share the blame."

"I have three sisters, but they didn't get into the same type of mischief I did." Her eyes twinkled with delight, and he felt an odd kinship with her. A feeling that, although they had only just met, they understood each other and could become good friends.

The server refilled the trays of bacon and pancakes and Jack stepped aside, allowing her to pick up a clean plate and serve herself.

After she'd gotten her food, Jack grabbed two plates, filling one with bacon for his brothers to share—or more likely fight over—and then added pancakes and scrambled eggs to a plate of his own. They stepped out of the way so others could access the buffet. "I'm Jack, by the way."

"Audrey." She looked him up and down. "I know who you are."

"You do?" He was both surprised and pleased. Although Jack had won numerous competitions and had the belt buckles and winning checks to prove his skill, Geoff was the superstar, recognized by people who didn't even follow rodeo, or any sport, for that matter.

"Of course. Everyone knows the Burris brothers." She looked at him and frowned, an expression that didn't appear to belong on her face. "Don't you know who *I* am?"

"Should I?" He shook his head as he tried to recall if they'd met before. But he knew they hadn't. He would never forget someone as beautiful and as magnetic as Audrey. The way his body was reacting to her nearness was something he'd never forget in a million years.

"I'm Audrey *Hawkins*." She emphasized her last name, and after a few blinks, the name rang a bell.

"You're one of the Hawkins Sisters."

The Hawkins Sisters were third-generation rodeo queens. Jack had yet to see them perform, but he'd heard all about them. They were getting a lot of press, most of which focused on their beauty, charm and fashion sense. As far as he was concerned, they were long on glitter and sparkle and short on what mattered. Talent.

"Yes. We haven't competed at the same rodeos yet, but it looks like we're finally going to get that chance. Your brother Geoff has been all over the place talking up Bronco. He made your town sound so wonderful. When we heard about the rodeo, we decided to check out the town for ourselves. We've only been here for a little while, but so far, so good. Bronco has been very welcoming," she said. "I've looked forward to meeting you and your brothers for the longest time. It's not often that there are two families competing together on the circuit."

That was one word for it. Jack wasn't a big fan of women rodeo riders, not since his good friend Janet had been paralyzed in a riding accident that he couldn't help believing a man would have walked away from. But at her small size and with her delicate body, she hadn't stood a chance.

Audrey was even more petite than Janet. The thought of her putting herself at risk bothered him, although he didn't know why.

He wasn't going to tell her that women didn't belong in rodeo when she obviously disagreed. Audrey was a grown woman who was going to make her own decision. He didn't have to become her friend and open himself up to worrying about her welfare either.

"Well, my brothers are waiting for their bacon and our food is getting cold. It was nice meeting you, Audrey. I guess I'll see you around."

He started toward his table, but she was faster than he was. She stepped around him, blocking his path. She might have been trying to look fierce, but she was much too cute and petite to pull it off. "Did I say something to offend you?"

"Not at all."

"Then why the cold shoulder all of a sudden?"

Wow. He hadn't expected her to call him on his behavior. Normally, people accepted the brush-off for what it was and went on with their lives. Audrey Hawkins was apparently no shrinking violet. Or perhaps she chose to ignore social cues when they didn't suit her purpose. "No cold shoulder. My brothers are waiting. Besides, we were holding up the line."

"Okay. Sure. I certainly don't want to keep your brothers waiting any longer. Good talking to you, Jack. Enjoy your food." Her voice dripped with sarcasm, and although she hadn't said the words, he had a feeling she'd wanted to say something along the line of *choke on your food.* She spun on her heels and strode across the floor to the table where three women he assumed were her sisters waited. Although they'd just met, a part of him regretted the way they'd parted. But that was ridiculous.

He wasn't destined to remain in anyone's life, and he wasn't meant for anything long-term. That was the way it was for a cowboy who spent more time on the highway than he did in one place. By the time he figured out the best restaurant to eat in and which places to avoid, it was time to move along to the next rodeo. The next town. And he was fine living that way. He didn't want to try to find the one woman who would be happy with his lifestyle. It still amazed him that Geoff had found a woman to love. But then, Stephanie, his soon to be sister-in-law, wasn't just any woman. She was a levelheaded nurse who made his brother happy. There weren't many women like her around.

Jack smiled as he thought of Geoff and Stephanie. They'd met when Geoff had gotten injured falling from the bleachers while doing a photo shoot at the Bronco Convention Center. He'd been rushed to the hospital where Stephanie worked. They'd fallen in love, and the rest, as the saying went, was history.

But then, his oldest brother had always led a charmed life. Not that Jack wanted to take away the good things from the guy's life. He didn't. And he certainly didn't begrudge Geoff anything that he'd earned. Jack knew his brother worked hard—you couldn't succeed in rodeo any other way. Jack admired his brother, had even worshipped him as a kid, but he was still working his hardest to dethrone Geoff as rodeo's biggest and most successful star. And he didn't need the distraction of a woman interfering with that.

"What took you so long?" Ross asked as Jack set the plate of bacon on the table.

"They had to get more food from the back," Jack said, dumping syrup onto his pancakes.

"Really? I thought it might have been that pretty lady you were talking to," Mike said, grinning. He grabbed a few slices of bacon and then bit into them all at once.

"You're lucky Mom wasn't here to see that," Ross said to Mike.

"See what?"

"You are such a barbarian. You have absolutely no couth."

"Do my table manners offend you, your highness?"

Jack shook his head. He was used to his brothers' antics. Although they all competed, they didn't always enter the same rodeo, so spending time together was a treat. At least, some of the time. Other times not so much. And this was turning into a not-so-much occasion.

"You'd better learn some etiquette before you start medical school," Ross said.

"No worries on that front. I know what fork to use. Besides, I'm going to be a surgeon, so I'll be using knives." Mike picked up his orange juice, lifted his pinkie in an exaggerated manner and then slurped loudly.

"You are so stupid," Ross said.

"I'm telling Mom you called me names," Mike said and then he and Ross burst into laughter.

"And to think, I actually missed you two knuckleheads," Jack said. "I don't know what I was thinking."

"Aww, we missed you, too," Ross said.

"So who was the girl?" Mike asked.

"What girl?"

"The one you were talking to. You were cheesing like you were getting your picture taken for a magazine cover."

"Nobody," Jack said. Mike and Ross simply stared at him and Jack knew he hadn't convinced his brothers. At times like this, he wished they didn't know each other so well. He blew out a breath. "Her name is Audrey Hawkins. She and her sisters compete in rodeo."

"The Hawkins Sisters. I've read about them," Mike said as he glanced over his shoulder for a look at the women. "They are gorgeous. I wouldn't mind getting to know them better while we're all in Bronco together."

Jack kicked his brother under the table, hopefully before one of them saw Mike looking in their direction. The last thing he wanted was for Audrey to think that he was talking about her. Okay, so he was talking about her, but not by choice. And to be fair, Ross and Mike were doing most of the talking. Jack had done his best to steer the conversation away from Audrey and her sisters. But even as he forced his brothers to return their attention back to their table, a part of him longed to take another glimpse at Audrey.

But he wouldn't.

"Why are you frowning?" Remi asked as Audrey set down her plate of pancakes and sausages.

"I didn't realize I was."

"Really? If looks could kill, someone would be pushing up daisies," Corinne, her baby sister, said.

"I'm fine."

"It must be the guy you were talking to. Did he say something to upset you?" Brynn asked, joining the conversation. At thirty, Brynn was three years older than Audrey and the oldest sister. She was a mother hen and very protective of her younger sisters.

"Who was he anyway? We didn't get a good look at his face. Do you know him?" Remi asked.

"Of course you would meet someone," Corinne added. "Does he live here or is he passing through?"

Audrey added butter and syrup to her pancakes and began to eat as her sisters talked over each other. This was the way the four of them communicated—doing a lot of talking and very little listening—so she was used to it. Besides, it worked for them. It was a gift that came from being sisters.

Brynn and Audrey were the biological children of their parents, Josie Hawkins and Steve Bristol. When Remi and Corinne were two and one, respectively, their mother was killed in a tragic riding accident. She'd been a close friend of Josie's and she and Steve adopted them. The four sisters were as close as could be, and unless people were familiar with the family, they didn't know that the youngest two were adopted.

But then, Hattie, Audrey's grandmother, had adopted four teenaged girls herself: Lisa, Suzie, Hollie, and Josie, Audrey's mother. Josie clearly felt that she was continuing as her own mother had taught her to do.

Once they'd exhausted their questions and fallen silent, Audrey took a sip of her now lukewarm coffee before answering. "I'm not upset. I'm fine. And the guy I was talking with is Jack Burris."

"Geoff Burris's brother?"

"One and the same," Audrey said wryly.

"Oh, he's cute," Remi said.

"Beauty is only skin-deep. He's a jerk."

"But one you concede is good-looking," Corinne said as if she'd made a great point instead of stating the obvious.

"What part of 'he's a jerk' did you miss?" Brynn said, saving Audrey the trouble. "No matter how handsome a man is, his personality matters more. Character counts."

"What's bugging you?" Corinne asked.

"Nothing," Brynn said. "I just don't want any of you to fall under some guy's spell just because he's been blessed with good genes."

"Or looks good in jeans," Remi added with a laugh.

"Anyway," Audrey said as Brynn rolled her eyes, "Jack is good-looking. I'm not denying that. But when I told him who I was, he got all distant."

"Oh."

Even Remi seemed disappointed by that statement. Remi was a romantic from the top of her head to the soles of her feet. But even she wouldn't tolerate someone who didn't think the Hawkins Sisters belonged, no matter how gorgeous he was.

"He's not the first man who has an issue with rodeo queens. How many times have we encountered men who don't respect us or our ability to do our jobs? Too many to count, right?" Audrey asked. "So I'm not going to let his attitude get under my skin. Nor am I going to spend another minute thinking about him. And I'm certainly not going to waste time talking about him when I could be enjoying this delicious food and spending time talking with my equally beautiful and talented sisters."

"Agreed," Brynn said, lifting her apple juice in a toast before taking a swallow.

"While you were getting your food, we were talking about Bronco. What do you think about this town?" Corinne asked.

"I like it," Audrey said honestly. "At least, what I've seen of it. The downtown has a lot of nice shops and restaurants. And the people seem friendly. And although Doug's is well off the beaten path, I like it. It's a nice welcoming bar-slash-restaurant. How do you guys feel about the town?"

"Same. It's everything Geoff Burris said it was. It might actually be some place we could settle down," Brynn said.

"Now wait a minute. We haven't been in town long enough to make that decision. It's going to take more than a good brunch to get me to go that far," Remi said. "I said I like it, not that I want to live here forever."

"We spend a lot of time on the road. I'm just thinking that we might want to have a home base. That's all."

"We have a home base. Houston, Texas. Where our mother lives."

"There's no need to argue. I'm finished eating. Do any of you want more, or are you ready to leave?" Audrey said.

Her sisters looked at each other. "We're done."

Audrey wiped her mouth and then stood. They'd paid for their food when they'd arrived, so they shoved their chairs up to the scarred table and added a generous tip to the jar on the bar. As they left, Audrey couldn't help but glance over at the table where she'd seen Jack and his brothers. Her eyes met his briefly and she frowned and looked away.

Jack Burris had gotten distant when he'd realized who she was, which was too bad. She'd enjoyed talking with him earlier. But she'd get over the disappointment. After all, he wasn't the first cowboy to dismiss a Hawkins Sister.

And that was reason enough to keep her distance.

Chapter Two

"Meeting in the living room," Corinne said, poking her head into Audrey's bedroom. They were going to be in Bronco for a few weeks, so rather than stay at a hotel, they'd found a house to rent.

The four-bedroom, two-and-a-half-bath Colonial their real estate agent had found was located on the Valley part of town. The houses here were older and the rooms a bit smaller than the ones in Bronco Heights, but once they'd taken a look at the pictures online, they'd all agreed that the charming two-story was perfect for them.

"I'll be right there," Audrey said, rising from

the cozy window seat. The sisters believed in being fair in all things, so rather than choose rooms by birth order, they'd drawn numbers out of a hat. Audrey had been last, but remarkably she'd gotten the best room. Sure, it was the smallest and the farthest away from the bathroom that she and Corinne shared, but it had a charming nook overlooking the backyard where she could sit and dream.

She jogged down the stairs and into the living room where her sisters were gathered. "What's up?"

"We're discussing our upcoming schedule and some invitations we've received," Brynn said. Brynn was the unofficial manager of the group. She was incredibly organized and did her best to find good opportunities for the Hawkins Sisters. She also made sure they were fairly compensated and received the billing they deserved.

"Are any of them new rodeos?" Remi asked.

"A couple. There's a new one in Wyoming that sounds interesting. And another one not too far from here later in the month. And there's one that doesn't sound so good. I'm inclined to tell them no, but I thought I'd check with you first."

Brynn went into detail about the three rodeos and the rest of the sisters agreed with her assessment. "So yes to two and no to the other?"

They all nodded. "I'll get back with them and give them each our decisions."

"Sounds good."

"Speaking of good," Remi said with a mischievous grin, "I've been thinking a little bit more about Jack Burris."

"Oh, no," Brynn said, shaking her head.

"Why?" Audrey asked. She should have known Remi was too much of a romantic to let the thing with Jack Burris go for long.

"Did he actually say that he didn't think women should participate in rodeo?"

"Not in so many words," Audrey admitted. "But I know the type."

"I looked him up on the internet," Remi said quickly. "The pictures of him are something else. And he comes across really well in his interviews. I think you should give him a chance before you write him off."

"I agree," Corinne added.

"You cannot be serious," Brynn said. "There's no reason for Audrey to go chasing after him. Or any man, for that matter. If he's interested, he should pursue her."

"I have no intention of chasing him," Audrey said. She knew her worth. And if she'd thought about him more times than she could count over the past twenty-four hours? Well, that didn't mean she was going to do anything foolish.

"But if you should run into him," Remi said, "there's no reason to turn and walk in the opposite direction."

"Audrey," Brynn said, putting her hands on her hips. "Don't you look him up or track him down. Period."

Brynn's cell phone rang at that moment, saving Audrey the need to repeat herself. She wasn't interested in Jack Burris. He might have been an unwelcome guest in her thoughts, and an uninvited star of her dreams, but she had no intention of letting him be a part of her life. He'd made it clear what he thought about her and she wasn't interested in educating him about women in the rodeo, including the illustrious women in her family. He could continue to be as biased and close-minded as he wanted to be. As long as he did it far away from her.

Brynn's phone rang one more time. She glanced at it and then hit the button to dismiss the call.

A few moments later, Audrey's cell phone rang. "Hey, it's Chuck Carter, the manager of the Bronco Convention Center," she said, reading the caller ID. She pressed the button to answer the call.

"Hi. Audrey?"

"Yes."

"It's Chuck Carter. I've been trying to reach Brynn, but I haven't been able to catch up with her."

"You don't say." Audrey glanced at her older sister. "Well, you've reached me. What can I do for you?"

"I'm hoping that the Hawkins Sisters have time in your schedule to shoot some promotional videos and photos for the upcoming rodeo."

"I think we might be able to manage that. When do you need us to stop by?"

"How does tomorrow sound? Does noon work for you?"

"Let me check with my sisters and get back to you. Okay?"

"It sounds perfect." Audrey ended the conversation and relayed the details to her sisters.

"The promotion sounds like a good idea," Corinne said. "The more people who know about us, the better."

"I don't know," Brynn said, dragging out the words.

"What's not to know?" Audrey asked. "Corinne is right. Publicity is always a good thing. I say we listen to what he has to say and then make our decision. We don't want to talk ourselves out of an opportunity before we even know what the offer is."

Brynn sighed. "Fine. I'll listen. Now, if that's all, I suggest we adjourn this meeting."

The sisters looked around and then nodded. The meeting was over.

Brynn rose and swept from the room.

"What's wrong with her?" Remi asked.

"Who knows? Maybe she's not feeling well," Corinne suggested.

"Hopefully she'll be back to her usual self by tomorrow," Audrey said. This was an opportunity to show Jack Burris that the Hawkins Sisters belonged in rodeo just as much as he and his brothers did. After all, the Burrises were local. Chuck could have called them and asked if they'd wanted to be featured in the promotion. But he hadn't. He'd called her and her sisters. She could just imagine Jack's expression when he saw the ads starring the Hawkins Sisters. She only wished she could be there to see the shocked look on his face. But since she had no intention of ever seeing him again, her imagination would have to do.

The next afternoon, Audrey and her sisters drove to the convention center on the outskirts of town. As they stepped inside, Chuck Carter came over to greet them. He was smiling broadly, as if he was delighted by their mere presence. A definite change from Jack Burris's negativity. And why was she wasting yet more time thinking about him? Generally when she decided that someone wasn't worth the time of day, she no longer gave them a second thought. Yet here she was, two days after she'd met Jack, and she was still unable to keep him out of her mind. She'd never admit it to another soul—heck, she hated admitting it to herself—but he'd starred in her dreams again last night.

She'd tossed and turned in her queen bed for hours, unable to get his dismissive attitude from her mind. When she'd finally fallen asleep, visions of him had invaded her mind. Even now, she recalled how good he'd looked that morning at brunch. Dressed in his jeans with his belt buckle that he'd obviously won in a rodeo event, and a blue-plaid shirt that had clung to his muscular chest and shoulders, he'd been the best-looking man she'd laid eyes on in quite some time. It had taken monumental effort to focus on what Jack had been saying.

His gorgeous smile had been so welcoming and warm, and for one moment in time, Audrey had believed they could become more than friends. The connection between them had been strong. She knew he'd felt it, too. But that was before his good humor had vanished when she'd told him who she was. What was it about men that made them go from rational people to jerks the second they realized that a woman could ride and rope just as skillfully as a man?

"Are you listening?" Remi asked.

Audrey nodded and shoved all thoughts of Jack Burris from her mind. He had no business there anyway. She couldn't control her dreams, but she could certainly master her thoughts.

"So how about a short tour?" Chuck asked, his eyes focused on Brynn. Clearly, he knew she was the Hawkins sister that he needed to win over.

"I don't know—" Brynn started to say when Corinne cut her off.

"We'd love to see everything. That way we'll be familiar with the site when the rodeo begins."

Brynn frowned and then nodded. Audrey had no idea why her sister was behaving this way, but getting the lay of the land was a good idea.

Chuck took the lead, showing them every nook and cranny of the building. When he finished the tour, they were once more in the auditorium. "Now that you've seen everything, I want to talk to you about my idea.

"You already know I'm a big fan of the Hawkins Sisters. In fact, I'm a fan of your entire family. I wish I could have your grandmother as well as your mother and aunts in the rodeo, but since that's not possible, I'm thrilled to have Josie's children here."

Audrey smiled at the mention of her mother. She and her sisters were third-generation rodeo stars. Her grandmother Hattie Hawkins was in her seventies now, but in her time, she'd been a huge star and a main attraction on the rodeo circuit. She'd always gotten top billing. She'd adopted her four daughters when they were teenagers. She'd taught them well and they'd traveled the rodeo circuit with her for years, performing as the Hawkins Sisters. They were all in their fifties now, with families of their own. Audrey was pleased that Chuck was well aware of their lineage and didn't mistake them as some new-to-the-game act.

"We're thrilled to be here," Corinne said.

"Last year we had our inaugural Mistletoe Rodeo."

"We heard about it," Brynn said.

"It was an enormous success. So successful that we're doing it again this Christmas. It's also part of the reason that we've organized the smaller event later this month to support Bronco tourism. We want to emphasize that rodeo is a family affair and encourage parents to bring their children. It occurred to me that we have two families of rodeo in town right now—the Burris brothers, who were born and raised here in Bronco, and the Hawkins Sisters. We'd like to feature you in our ads, playing up the family angle."

"That sounds interesting. We'd need to iron out the details before we make a firm commitment," Brynn said.

"Naturally. This is still a business deal, after all," Chuck said. "I don't know how this will figure in your decision-making process, but we'll be donating part of the admission fees to a local charity. The Burris brothers have already said yes."

Remi and Corinne smiled at each other and then glanced over at Audrey. Despite trying to play it cool, her cheeks began to burn.

"Is that right?" Remi asked.

"Yes. They should be here any moment to discuss things," Chuck said. "In fact, here they are now."

Audrey spun around and her heart began to race as she looked at Jack. Although he was walking beside two of his brothers, she barely noticed them. She couldn't keep her eyes off him. Dressed in dark blue jeans, a Western-styled shirt that clung to his shoulders and a black cowboy hat, he was a sight to behold. Too bad those good looks were wasted on someone who didn't respect what she did.

"Welcome," Chuck said, holding out his arms as the Burris brothers drew near. "I was just talking about you."

"I hope it was good," one of Jack's brothers said with a grin.

"I only know good things about you," Chuck said.

"Have you met?" Chuck asked, looking between them.

"No," that same brother answered. His smile

was friendly as he glanced at Audrey and her sisters. She noticed that his eyes lingered on Corinne a bit longer and his smile broadened. "I'm Mike Burris and these are my brothers, Jack and Ross. And you ladies must be the Hawkins Sisters. It's a pleasure to meet all of you."

Chuck stepped forward and quickly introduced everyone. After the greetings were exchanged, they all turned to listen to Chuck. Somehow during the introductions, they had moved around, and Audrey was now standing beside Jack. They were so close that they bumped into each other.

"Pardon me," he said. His deep voice struck a chord inside her, and despite insisting that she wasn't attracted to him, she shivered. She drew in a deep breath and caught the subtle scent of his cologne. She didn't ordinarily pay attention to scents—she spent too much time around men who smelled like horses to bother. But she did know that she liked it and the way it smelled on him. That troublesome thought made her even more annoyed at him.

"Don't worry about it," she said, taking two steps away from him and his attractive scent.

She looked over and caught Remi and Corinne staring at her. Great. Just what she didn't need. Her sisters were wonderful and she loved them to pieces, but they were always seeing romance in everything. They were the two biggest matchmakers on the face of the earth. Not for themselves or each other, mind you, but for everyone else. And now they had her in their sights. Did they really believe she and Jack Burris would make a good couple? They couldn't be more wrong.

"I know you ladies haven't decided to commit to the ad campaign for the rodeo," Chuck began, breaking into her thoughts, "but if you do, we would want to do a joint campaign that would involve photographing the two families together."

"That makes sense," Mike said, and Remi and Corinne nodded in agreement.

Audrey kept her eyes focused on Chuck. She didn't want to take pictures with Jack, memorializing their meeting. She wanted to pretend that they had never met. Suddenly she didn't believe that all publicity was good.

"What kind of pictures are you talking about?" Jack asked.

"Oh, you know, the usual kind," Chuck said. "A few pictures of you all together. And maybe a couple of you paired off and some such. We'd let the photographer come up with the shots that he thinks are best."

"Just as long as nobody is standing on top of the bleachers," Ross said and his brothers nodded.

"I don't get it. Why would that be a problem? Don't tell me you big strong cowboys are afraid of heights?" Audrey's voice dripped with sarcasm as she stared at Jack.

"Not at all," he answered smoothly. "Our brother Geoff was injured last year when he fell from the top of those bleachers right there. He ended up needing surgery. We'd like to avoid a repeat of that incident if we could."

"So would I," Chuck added.

"Oh, I heard about that," Corinne said. "I'm glad that he's fully recovered."

Audrey had heard about that injury, too, and acknowledged that the Burris men had a legitimate reason for being wary. But people were injured in the rodeo all the time—that was the risk they took—but they still competed every night. But who expected to get injured so badly in a photo shoot that they required surgery?

"That's very kind of you," Mike said.

Audrey might not like Jack, but she had to admit that his brothers seemed to be nice people. At least they hadn't sneered at doing joint publicity. She would prefer not to do the campaign with Jack, but even she knew that it was a good idea and would raise the Hawkins Sisters' profile. Although the Hawkins Sisters were well-known in rodeo circles, Geoff Burris, and by extension his brothers, was well-known in *all* sports circles. This was an opportunity she and her sisters couldn't let slip by, despite how badly she wanted to stay away from Jack.

Jack listened with one ear as everyone discussed the possible campaign and different ways to make it successful. Although he nodded when appropriate, he was distracted by Audrey's presence.

Their encounter the other day had been brief and had ended on a sour note, but he hadn't been able to put her out of his mind. At the oddest moments, he would hear her laughter or picture her smile. She was so incredibly beautiful. Even though she couldn't be more than five foot three or four, she was a dynamic person who packed a strong personality. There was nothing petite about her attitude. He liked her confidence, and under other circumstances, he would have been interested in seeing her while he was in town. But she was a rodeo queen, which made her off-limits.

"Why are you staring at me?" she hissed, leaning in close so only he could hear her.

"I didn't realize that I was."

"Well, you are, so knock it off."

"Or what?" He wasn't one to engage in immature challenges, so his childish behavior surprised him. "They're my eyes, so I can look where I want."

"You really are a jerk."

"Am I?"

She looked away and he was immediately filled with remorse. She was right. He was being a jerk. There was no excuse for that. "You're right. I apologize. I didn't know that you and your sisters were going to be a part of this promotion. Seeing you here took me by surprise. But that is no excuse to treat you badly. I hope you can forgive me."

She nibbled on her full bottom lip as if trying to decide whether he was being sincere.

He held his breath and met her gaze, hoping she would see the truth in his eyes. He couldn't explain why her opinion mattered to him, but it did.

Finally, she nodded. "Apology accepted. This time."

"Not to worry. There won't be a second." His parents had raised him better than that. And he didn't have an imaginary friend to blame.

That seemed to please her because she smiled and her brown eyes sparkled. He realized then that conversation had stopped. When he glanced up, everyone was staring at him and Audrey. From the smug grins on his brothers' faces, he could easily imagine what they were thinking. They thought there was something romantic brewing between him and Audrey. They couldn't be more wrong.

Sure, she was beautiful. She might be petite, but she was one-hundred-percent sexy woman.

There was something about the way her faded jeans caressed her slender curves and the way her pink-and-green top hugged her breasts that made her stand out. Even wearing scuffed cowboy boots, she was movie-star glamorous. But it wasn't her body alone that had him wanting to spend more time with her. It was her personality. What was it about Audrey Hawkins that had him wanting to get close to her? He didn't know, but he needed to get a grip.

The best thing for his peace of mind would be to keep his distance. He and his brothers had already agreed to the photo shoot, so there was no backing out. When they gave their word, they kept it, so he didn't want to flake out now. Especially in his hometown.

Besides, this was his opportunity to step out of his brother's shadow. To show the world who he was and what he could do—apart from being Geoff Burris's younger brother. And if accomplishing that meant doing a promo with the Hawkins Sisters, so be it. He'd set his personal feelings about women in rodeo aside. He just had to make sure he didn't develop personal feelings for Audrey.

Chapter Three

The next day Audrey walked into the convention center and looked around. After discussing the matter, she and her sisters had agreed that the promotion was something they couldn't say no to. They were supposed to meet here in about twenty minutes, but since Audrey had been in the area, she'd decided to stop in now.

She'd spent the morning looking around Bronco. Although there was much she hadn't seen, there was something about this town that appealed to her and had her taking a second look. While she'd wandered around, she'd seen a few restaurants, numerous boutiques that looked right up her alley, and hangout spots she'd like to explore. The people she'd encountered at Bronco Java and Juice had been welcoming and friendly.

She and her sisters spent plenty of time on the road, and whenever they were in one town for more than a few days, Audrey liked to wander around and get a feel for the town. She enjoyed meeting the townspeople and going to spots far off the beaten path, like Doug's.

Tourist traps were okay every once in a while, and she'd picked up quite a few souvenirs on the circuit, but in her estimation, that wasn't the way to really get to know a place. That knowledge only came from going where the locals went. She didn't know why that mattered to her so much, and she'd struggled to explain the inclination to her sisters and parents, but she had this need to know the places they traveled to. Audrey wasn't sure what she was looking for, or if she was looking for anything at all, but she knew she'd recognize it when she saw it.

Her sisters weren't here yet, but since she was early, she hadn't expected them to be. In her experience, they would arrive exactly on schedule. Not one minute earlier, nor one minute later, than the agreed-upon time.

Audrey set the garment bag filled with outfits that she'd selected for the photo shoot on a bleacher and then looked around, imagining the space as it would be for the rodeo. She could practically smell the horses and feel the dirt under her feet. She could almost hear the crowd cheering as she broke her own roping record. She smiled broadly at the image.

"What's so funny?"

She jumped and turned at the sound of Jack Burris's voice. When she looked at him, her stomach did a silly little flip-flop. He was dressed in jeans and a white button-down shirt, a black garment bag slung over one shoulder. With his cowboy hat dipped low over one eye, he looked sexy and dangerous all at once. His lips spread in a slow smile and shivers raced down her spine. He was too good-looking for her peace of mind. If she knew what was good for her, she'd keep her distance from him.

When he continued to stare at her, she realized she hadn't answered his question. There was keeping your distance and then there was being struck speechless. "Inside joke."

He nodded. "And if you tell me, you'll have to kill me, I suppose."

She laughed. "That's a bit of an overreaction for a joke, don't you think? I just don't believe you'll think it's funny."

"So you're saying you have a strange sense of humor?"

"*Quirky* is the word I would use, but yeah, my

sense of humor wouldn't be characterized as run-of-the-mill."

"I have to admit that mine isn't either."

He smiled and Audrey found herself getting lost in it. He was acting like the Jack he'd been when they'd first met at Doug's. The Jack that had been so attractive.

"What do you have in that garment bag?" he asked, nodding toward the bleacher. "Or is that a state secret?"

"The joke wasn't a state secret. But as far as my outfits go, you'll have to wait to see me in them."

His eyes swept over her body and heat surged through her. "I'll look forward to that."

"But there's no reason for you to not show me what you plan to wear," she said, reaching for his garment bag.

He held the bag out of her reach. "Oh, no, my pretty friend. If I have to wait, so do you."

Did Jack think she was pretty? He looked shocked by his words, so clearly the comment had been spontaneous. She felt herself blushing and her gaze flew to his. His looked intense. Deep. Dark. There was some emotion there, but she hadn't known him long enough, nor well enough, to decipher it. He blinked and whatever she'd seen there was gone and once more his eyes looked friendly.

The flash from a camera surprised them and they jumped and spun around as if they'd been caught doing something wrong. That was ridiculous. They'd only been talking. Okay, maybe they'd been doing a bit of flirting, too, but they were each single, so they were entitled.

A man with a camera slung around his neck by a thick black strap snapped a couple more pictures of them. Then he released the camera, picked up a video camera and started to film them. "Don't mind me. Keep on with what you're doing."

Audrey glanced at Jack, who looked at her and then shrugged one of his massive shoulders. He took a step in the man's direction, partially shielding Audrey from view. "Who are you?"

"Sorry." The man turned off his camera and then held out his hand. He shook Jack's hand first and then offered his hand to Audrey. "Willie Mayfield. Owner of Picture This Photography Studio." He pulled business cards from his pocket and gave one to each of them. "Chuck Carter hired me to take pictures and film some commercials for the Bronco Summer Family Rodeo. I figured since you're both here already, we'll start with the two of you and then add your siblings when they arrive."

Apparently he felt like he'd explained everything well enough and that they'd consented to his plan because he began to film them again.

Not entirely comfortable with the photographer's presence, Audrey stepped closer to Jack. The heat from his body reached out and wrapped around her, at once both comforting and unsettling. He was a bundle of contradictions. But then, perhaps the confusion wasn't coming from him, but rather her response to him.

"What is it?" Jack asked, even though she hadn't said a word.

"Does this seem normal to you?"

"You're asking me?"

"Yes. Of the two of us, you're currently more famous. And this is your hometown. Is this the way people normally do things here?"

She must have said the right thing because his eyes lit up and he smiled. He had a dimple in his right cheek, and it made an appearance, temporarily distracting her. Thinking straight was a challenge when Jack Burris was around, especially when he turned on his abundant charm as he was doing now.

"I spend about as much time on the rodeo circuit as you do, so although I was born and raised here, I can't speak to what happens in Bronco. As far as Willie goes, let's follow his lead. But if he makes you feel the slightest bit uncomfortable, let me know and I'll get rid of him."

"Let's be clear, you don't mean in the *have to kill him way*, right?"

Jack froze momentarily and then threw back his head and laughed. It was a deep, robust sound that was contagious, and she found herself laughing along with him. After a moment, he wiped a tear from his eye, a hint of a smile tugging at his lips. "Yeah, it's safe to say that we won't have to stuff a dead body into our garment bags and bury him in my parents' backyard."

"What do you mean *we*?"

"Oh, so I take it you won't be my partner in crime?"

"You got that right. I'm not sure you can get away with it. And make no mistake about it, I'm not built for prison."

He chuckled. "Not to worry. As small as you are, one of your sisters could smuggle you out of your cell in her purse."

She punched him in the arm. His muscle was hard as a rock, and she had to keep herself from shaking out her hand. "I'm not that small. It's just that the world is filled with you six-foot-tall giants."

"Yeah, you are that small. But what you lack in size, you definitely make up for in personality."

"I'm not sure… Was that a compliment? Or was it an insult?"

"You have to ask?"

"Oh, yeah. I'm not sure where you're coming from, Jack Burris."

"You really are something."

"Again. Compliment or insult?"

He blew out a breath and raised his eyes to the ceiling as if searching for help. For some reason, giving him a hard time thrilled her. She liked the way his brown eyes had widened with shock before he burst into laughter. She enjoyed seeing him squirm with confusion and doubt. Jack was so confident of his place in the world, it was satisfying to be able to knock him off-balance. It was only fair since he knocked her off her center whenever he was around. Every time they met, he'd been cool as a cucumber while she'd been flustered.

He placed his hands on her shoulders and then leaned closer, looking her dead in the eyes. "Compliments. They're compliments, Audrey."

And just like that, with his touch, he'd knocked her off-kilter and she'd lost the battle of self-control. She swayed on her feet, leaning closer to him. For a moment, she was unable to think clearly, much less speak. He was just so darn attractive. So distracting. So…smooth. Maybe too smooth? Just how often had he used this line or one similar to it? Given the reputation of cowboys and his good looks, she had no doubt that he had more than his share of buckle bunnies circling him, trying to get his attention. She needed to keep her wits about her and not let herself be swept away.

She forced herself to step back before Jack realized just how lethal his smile was and how much his nearness affected her. "Then I accept your compliments in the spirit they were extended."

He nodded. "Now, if we could just get that guy to stop taking pictures of us."

Audrey had been so caught up in Jack's nearness that she'd actually forgotten the photographer was there. Now that Jack mentioned it, why was the guy taking pictures? The photo shoot hadn't even started yet.

"Are we late?"

At the sound, Audrey looked away to find her sisters entering the center. They were lugging their bags over their shoulders and looking around. Audrey checked her watch. "No. You're right on time. We just need to wait for Jack's brothers to arrive."

Remi raised her eyebrows and her eyes twinkled with mischief. Corinne grinned and poked Remi in the side. It took a moment for Audrey to realize what she had said. She'd referred to Mike and Ross as *Jack's brothers*, emphasizing their connection to him. Naturally her two younger sisters would pick up on that. They were way too smart for their own good.

"We're here now," Mike said, stepping inside and saving Audrey from Remi and Corinne's teasing. At least for the time being. There wasn't a smidge of doubt that they would mention her slip of the tongue later. They'd already spent hours trying to convince her to give Jack a chance before kicking him to the curb. Somehow they had become Jack's biggest champions. Thankfully Brynn hadn't jumped on that bandwagon. In fact, she hadn't said another word about Jack. Once she'd made her opinion known, the matter was settled for her.

Remi, her fun-loving sister, had tried to tempt her by pointing out all the fun she could have with Jack. As if Remi could tell that someone was fun just by looking at him. And Corinne had continued to argue on Jack's behalf, pointing out how much Audrey had enjoyed talking to him at Doug's. That was true. But that had been before he'd revealed his narrow-minded ways.

"So what's the plan?" Ross asked.

Everyone turned to look at Willie, who introduced himself and distributed more business cards. "I'd like to start with pictures of all of you together. Then I'll take pictures of the Hawkins sisters and Burris brothers on your own. Finally, I'd like to take pictures of Jack and Audrey together."

"What?" Audrey blinked. He wanted to photograph her and Jack alone together? "Why?"

"Because I've been watching the two of you for the past twenty minutes and you've definitely got chemistry. We can use that vibe to our advantage. If you want to draw people to this event, the connection between the two of you is the best way to do it."

"I think it's a great idea," Corinne said.

Audrey glared at her baby sister, who smiled innocently. Corinne was lucky she was so cute and that everyone loved her.

"Sounds like a plan," Ross said as if it was all decided.

Audrey and Jack exchanged a long look. She hated that they were silently communicating, but she couldn't deny that they were on the same wavelength. At least about this. Besides, they were outnumbered and they knew it. Audrey sighed and Jack shrugged. He looked at the photographer. "Fine. Let's get this show on the road."

Audrey picked up her garment bag and then followed her sisters to the far end of the arena where a makeshift changeroom had been set up. Jack and his brothers headed to a similar setup in the other direction.

The changing area consisted of five seven-foot-tall folded panels lined next to each other to create a wall. There were four chairs behind the panels. The sisters dropped their bags onto the floor, sat down and began to remove their shoes. During their time in rodeo, they'd had to make do with all types of changing rooms, so they didn't blink an eye at this setup. There had been times when a dozen women were changing in a space of this size, so this felt like a palace. And it was more convenient than going all the way to the ladies' room.

Under other circumstances, Audrey wouldn't have hesitated, but there was something about knowing that Jack was on the other side of the arena stripping out of his clothes the same as she was that gave her pause.

Audrey felt a sharp poke in her side and jumped. "Are you going to sit there daydreaming or are you going to get changed?"

She looked into Brynn's eyes and nodded. "Right. Sorry."

"What's with you?"

"Nothing."

"I bet she's thinking about Jack," Corinne teased as she buttoned her yellow satin blouse with blue fringe.

"I sure hope not," Brynn said. "I thought we had agreed that she wasn't going to pursue him. If he's interested he should make the first move."

"We think she should give him a chance and not let one incident that she could have totally misinterpreted ruin a beautiful relationship," Remi said.

"Besides, he looked pretty into her a minute ago," Corinne added.

"*She* is sitting right here," Audrey pointed out. She jerked off her jeans and then pulled on her yellow satin skirt. "And I wasn't thinking about Jack or anyone else. If you must know, I was thinking about other rodeos and changing rooms."

"Well, that's boring," Remi said, settling her hat on her head and then turning so Corinne could adjust it before returning the favor for her sister. "I prefer my scenario, so that's what I'm going with."

"Whatever floats your boat," Audrey replied. She straightened her clothes and then put on her hat. Since there wasn't a mirror around, they inspected each other's clothes and makeup. Once they were satisfied that they were all camera ready, they went back to the center of the arena, where the photographer awaited.

Showtime.

"What's up with you and Audrey?" Mike asked as he fastened the buttons on his shirt.

Jack pretended not to hear his brother as he shoved his feet back into his boots. He would have preferred to take candid shots in his daily wardrobe, but Chuck had insisted that they wear their rodeo garb to look like authentic cowboys. Jack didn't understand how a costume would be more authentic than the clothes he wore every day, but then, promotion wasn't his job.

"You know he's not talking to me," Ross said, nudging Jack's shoulder with his own.

"I'm ignoring him as the pest that he is, hoping that he'll take the hint."

Mike laughed. If anything ever bothered him, Jack and his brothers had yet to discover it. Mike had always been happy-go-lucky, a smile permanently affixed to his face.

"Ah, well, if there's nothing going on, maybe I'll ask her out. She is pretty cute," Mike said.

"You'd better stay away from her," Jack snapped.

Ross and Mike laughed, and Jack realized he'd stepped into some sort of trap. Mike's smile broadened. "So there is something going on."

"No, there isn't," Jack denied.

"Do you want there to be?"

"What I want is for the two of you to stop being so annoying, but I guess there's no chance of that happening."

"I think we might have gotten too close to the truth," Ross said.

"What truth? Do I think Audrey is beautiful? Of course I do. Does that mean I'm suddenly going to fall head over heels in love with her and ask her to marry me or some such nonsense? No.

Now, if you two goofs are ready, let's go get our pictures taken so we can get out of here."

"Yes, sir, boss sir," Mike said, standing at attention and saluting.

Shaking his head and ignoring his brothers' laughter as they followed him, Jack walked out of the dressing area. He glanced toward the other end of the arena just as the Hawkins sisters were walking to the center, and his mouth fell open. Although there were four women dressed in identical formfitting yellow blouses and skirts with matching boots and hats, his eyes were drawn to Audrey.

She was a vision. He'd seen many beautiful women in his life, but none had come close to looking as breathtaking as Audrey did now. As she drew closer, all he could do was stare.

"You might want to close your mouth there," Ross said as she sidled up to Jack. "Wouldn't want to swallow a fly."

Jack snapped his mouth shut, but he couldn't look away. It was as if Audrey had magical powers and had somehow cast a spell on him. Just how did one break out of an enchantment? And did he even want to be free?

"Okay," Willie said. "Now that everyone is here, let's take a few pictures."

He instructed everyone on where to stand and how he wanted them to pose. Since there were four women and three men, he alternated a Hawkins and a Burris and placed the smallest person front and center. That meant Audrey was close enough to see, but just out of his reach.

"You know, I think it's a bit discriminatory to always make me stand in front," Audrey said after the second outfit change. "I mean my sisters get to stand next to all these handsome men and I have to stand alone."

"Nobody told you to be born short," Brynn said, tossing her black hair over her shoulders. She was the tallest of the sisters, and with her willowy body, she could have been a fashion model. For all of her good looks, she wasn't the one who made Jack's heart beat faster. He'd been standing beside her for thirty minutes and had felt absolutely nothing.

Everyone laughed.

"Maybe if you think tall thoughts, you'll grow a few inches," Corinne said with a cheeky grin. Although she wasn't as tall as Brynn, she was a few inches taller than Audrey.

"Don't make fun of Audrey," Remi said. "It's not her fault she stopped growing. You might be small, but don't forget you're mighty."

Jack wanted to jump in and tell them to stop teasing Audrey, but she laughed, clearly amused. Apparently, this was a familiar family joke between the sisters, much like the jokes he shared with his brothers. Still, he wouldn't mind if she traded places with Brynn for a while.

"Maybe we can get a crate for her," Jack found himself suggesting.

"Hey," Audrey said, "I'm not that short."

"That won't be necessary," Willie said. He'd been snapping pictures the entire time they'd been talking. And Jack couldn't be sure because his attention had been on Audrey, but he thought the photographer had been taking videos as well. Jack had been in lots of photo shoots in the past, but he'd never had this much fun. Nor had he been as eager and curious to see the final pictures.

"Why not?" Audrey asked.

"Because we're going to take pictures of you and Jack together, remember?"

"Ooh," everyone hooted and laughed.

"Aren't you special?" Ross said. "But I think I should be the one to pose with Audrey. After all, I'm much better-looking than Jack could ever dream of being."

"Yeah, but I'm better-looking than you both," Mike chimed in.

"Knock it off," Jack said. Brynn was standing between him and Ross, making it impossible to punch his brother in the arm the way he wanted to. And Mike was even farther away, standing between Corinne and Remi, who seemed amused by the entire exchange.

His brothers only laughed. Sometimes he forgot how annoying they could be, but at times like this, it all came rushing back to him.

"That's it for these outfits," Willie said. "Change into the last ones and we'll be done."

They walked back to their dressing rooms. When Jack was sure they were out of earshot, he wheeled around to look at his brothers. "What is wrong with you two?"

"Well, my elbow is still hurting from where I was thrown last week in South Dakota, thanks for asking," Ross said. "You really are a great big brother. So caring."

"And I feel a headache coming on," Mike added. "I probably should have hydrated better. I have a bottle of water with me, so I'll take care of that now."

Jack shook his head, wondering if he could survive prison. But then, maybe he could find a good hiding place for their bodies. "You guys have missed your calling. You're wasting your talents competing. You should be rodeo clowns."

Jack knew he shouldn't let his brothers get to him—they would continue needling him as long as they got a reaction—but he couldn't help it. The idea of one of them taking his place in the photo shoot with Audrey rubbed him the wrong way. Inhaling deeply, he reminded himself that he would be the one beside Audrey, not one of them. He'd been reluctant before, but now he couldn't wait.

The two families laughed and joked as they posed for the last set of photographs. Willie had been shooting candid videos as well, so by the time he'd told them he'd gotten enough pictures of the group, Jack's brothers and Audrey's sisters were ready to go. They made a mad dash for the changing areas while he and Audrey waited for further instructions.

"Are you up for this now, or do you need a break?" Jack asked her.

"I'm ready to do it now."

"Okay. Just checking." Jack didn't know why he felt so protective of her when she'd proved that she could take care of herself, but he did.

Willie looked at them. "I would prefer to have shots of the two of you dressed in your street clothes."

"Really?" Audrey asked. She sounded slightly disappointed. Jack had to admit that she did look particularly sexy in her red dress with white fringe, white hat and white boots. Of the three outfits the sisters had worn today, this was his favorite. It clung to each of her curves, giving Jack ideas he shouldn't be entertaining.

"Yes."

"You're the professional. If you think jeans and a shirt is the way to go, then I'll be right back."

She turned to leave and Jack grabbed her hand. She spun back around and looked at him, her big brown eyes a mixture of curiosity and confusion. Jack tugged her closer and leaned down to whisper in her ear. "I don't know what Willie is thinking, but you look sexy as hell in that outfit. You're definitely worthy of having your very own photo shoot."

The smile she gave him made the blood pulse in his veins and his heart began thumping so hard he could practically hear it. "Thanks. You don't look so bad yourself. But since he is the professional, I suggest we change."

Mike and Ross waited for him to change so they could take his clothes home for him. "Thanks," he said, handing over his garment bag. Sometimes they weren't so bad, he supposed.

Audrey and her sisters returned to the main area at the same time Jack and his brothers did.

"Have fun," Remi said, waving and grinning mischievously.

"Thanks for taking my clothes home," Audrey said.

Brynn waved a hand in response as she and Corinne followed Remi out the door. A minute later, Jack and Audrey were alone with Willie.

"Where do you want us to stand?" Jack asked.

"Give me a minute," Willie said from behind his camera. "Just talk amongst yourselves."

"I hope he has us pose by the bleachers," Audrey said.

"Why? You know how I feel about that."

"So I can stand on one and be taller than you. In fact, I'm going over there now."

"I don't think so," he said.

Audrey laughed. "How are you going to stop me?"

She turned and started to run to the bleachers. Before he could give it a second thought, he'd pulled her into his arms and tossed her over his shoulder. Audrey was light as a feather and holding her was easy.

Even so, he paused. What had possessed him to pick her up this way? In most cases, he knew what he'd planned to do when he had a woman in his arms.

With Audrey? Not so much.

Chapter Four

Audrey felt the air whoosh out of her seconds before she burst into laughter. One minute she was dashing over to the bleachers and the next she was upside down, slung over Jack's shoulders. Ordinarily she wouldn't appreciate being tossed about like a sack of dirty laundry, but for some reason, she found the situation incredibly funny. Perhaps because she was so surprised by Jack's totally unexpected action.

While they'd been posing for pictures with their siblings, he'd been the stoic one. Willie had had to keep telling him to loosen up. Ross and Mike had teased him mercilessly and he'd eventually unwound. She didn't get it. She'd seen photos of Jack in magazines and he always seemed at ease in front of the camera. Now she wondered just how many shots the photographer had taken before he'd gotten those images.

The thought made her groan. She could be here all night.

"Are you okay?" Jack asked, setting her back on her feet just as quickly as he'd swooped her into his arms.

"I'm fine. Why?"

"You groaned. I thought you might be getting queasy."

"And you were worried that I might barf on your designer shirt? If I were you, I'd be worried about my boots." He jumped back, a shocked look on his face, and she started laughing again. "I'm joking. I'm made of sterner stuff than that."

"How should I know? I don't have sisters. And you look so…"

"So what? Delicate?"

He looked at her for a second before replying. "*Delicate* is the last word I'd use to describe you. You're…uh—well…"

"What word would you use?"

"Is there a word I can use that won't get me in trouble?"

She raised an eyebrow. "You tell me."

"I have no idea what words to use to describe you. Heck, the words might not even exist."

"I'm unique. An original. One of a kind."

He grinned mischievously. "You're indescribable."

"I'll accept that. Now, if you'll excuse me..." She turned and raced for the bleachers.

As she ran, she heard Jack's footsteps behind her, so she bobbed and weaved, determined to stay out of his grasp. She dodged his outstretched hand and reached the bleachers mere seconds before he did. Without pausing, she darted up two steps and then turned to look at him. He was standing with his hands on his hips, the pose emphasizing his broad shoulders and chest and the way they tapered to his six-pack abs and trim waist.

When she realized that she was ogling him, she forced her eyes up to meet his. He raised an eyebrow. Clearly, he'd noticed her inspection. Was he waiting to see how she rated him? If so, he was out of luck. He was going to have to get his ego stroked by some other woman.

She glanced over her shoulder. Willie had followed the two and was currently taking photos of them.

"I think we should take a few pictures over here," Audrey said. "That way, I'll be taller than Jack."

"You won't be taller than I am. I'll still be six feet and you'll still be five foot...what? Three?"

She shook her head. He was so literal. "I'm five-three and three-quarters, if you must know. Now come stand over here and pose. Show off those pretty teeth and that dimple."

"You think my teeth are pretty, do you?"

She laughed. "I never took you for the vain type, Jack."

"I'm not. But I'm not about to let a rare compliment from you slip by unremarked upon either."

"Was I supposed to be complimenting you? I didn't realize that was part of the deal."

"Clearly, you didn't read the small print. But don't worry, the compliments are supposed to be reciprocated, so I guess it's my turn to say something nice about your appearance." He rubbed his chin and stared at her for several seconds.

"Don't hurt yourself trying."

He grinned. "That's not the problem at all. I was actually trying to limit myself to one."

"Don't feel compelled to do that. The more, the merrier, I always say."

"I think that saying only applies to people and ribs."

"Ribs? Now that's a new one."

"Forgive me. I'm hungry and I could really go for some ribs at DJ's Deluxe."

"What's that?"

"Only the best place in town for fall-off-the-bone ribs. Don't tell me you haven't eaten there yet?"

"Okay, I won't."

"When we finish up here, I'll take you there for a late lunch." He shook his head. "That didn't come out right. What I meant to do was ask you if you would like to join me for lunch."

"Sounds great." She looked at Willie, who'd been filming away the entire time. She took a step down so that she was standing on the bottom bleacher. "Where do you want us to stand?"

"I've gotten some great shots of the two of you now. Really candid ones. But one or two posed ones will work, too."

"You've been taking pictures of us?" Jack asked, voicing the question before Audrey could. They'd been goofing around. She could only imagine how those pictures would turn out.

"Yep. And let me tell you, the chemistry between the two of you is off the charts. These pictures are going to be the best advertisement for the rodeo that we have. But since we're over here, let's get a shot with Audrey on the step and you beside her."

Jack rolled his eyes and Audrey made a face. When she realized what she'd done, she looked over at Willie. "You got that, didn't you?"

"Oh, yeah."

Jack roared as if it was the funniest thing he'd ever heard until he realized Willie had turned the camera on him. Then he sobered and came to stand beside her.

Audrey was suddenly aware of just how attractive Jack was. She longed to reach out and touch him, but that would be totally inappropriate. Not only that, Willie would probably capture that, too. Instead, she fiddled with the buttons on her blouse. When she realized what she was doing, she dropped her hands to her sides.

She inhaled deeply, hoping the breath would calm her. Instead of a relaxing breath, she got a whiff of Jack's enticing scent. It was a heavenly mixture of his unique aroma and his cologne. He smelled just as good today as he had at brunch the other day. Her eyes drifted closed for a moment, and when she opened them, Willie was snapping photos. She didn't even want to think of what he'd captured in her unguarded moment.

They posed for a few more shots. Audrey wasn't surprised that she felt a lot less relaxed now than when she was completely unaware that her picture was being taken.

After about thirty minutes, Willie lowered his camera. "It's a wrap. Thanks so much for your time. These are going to be great."

"Would it be possible for us to see the pictures

when they're done?" Jack asked. "And maybe even get a copy or two? If we like what we see."

"You're going to love what you see. And no, I don't have a problem with that. Give me your number and I'll give you a call and set up something." Willie grinned and tapped his camera. "There's magic here."

Jack and Audrey gave Willie their numbers and then said their goodbyes.

"So, are you up to having lunch with me?" Jack asked.

"Absolutely. After the way you described DJ's Deluxe, I can't wait."

They walked into the parking lot. Audrey spotted a fancy sports car before glancing over at her two-year-old Escape and then back. "Whew. Now that's what I call a car."

"You like it?"

"Uh, yeah. Do you even have to ask?"

"We can take my car and leave yours here. I'll drop you back after."

"Sounds like a plan." She rubbed her hand over the red car. "I don't suppose you'll let me drive this baby."

He shook his head. "I have no idea the kind of driver you are."

"True. But I'll drive her the way she was meant to be driven."

"That sounds like you're a speed demon."

"Don't tell me you drive like a little old lady. That would totally disrespect this car. This baby was meant to be driven fast."

"Would you believe me if I said I did?"

"Nope."

"I didn't think so."

Jack pressed the button on his key fob, disengaging the lock. He then opened the passenger door and held it so that she could get in. Audrey glanced up at him and smiled. "Thanks."

He touched the tip of his cowboy hat. "Absolutely, ma'am."

While he circled the front of the car, Audrey gave herself a stern talking to. She wasn't about to fall for Jack simply because he had a great sense of humor and a superior body. She had better sense than that. At least, she hoped she did.

Jack gave his name to the hostess and followed her to the table for two near the front windows.

He didn't bother with his menu. "I'm getting the large rib meal."

She put hers down. "I think I'll do the same."

"Do you think you can finish all of that?"

"Yep. In fact, I think I might like an appetizer, too."

"How about we split one?"

"Sounds good."

They gave their orders to the waitress, who was back right away with their beverages.

Audrey took a sip of her cola and then leaned back in her chair. She closed her eyes in apparent bliss. "That's refreshing."

Jack swallowed his drink and took the opportunity to look at Audrey—really look at her—while her eyes were closed. Her face was so beautiful. With high cheekbones, full lips and clear brown skin, she was exquisite. But more than being gorgeous, she was electric. Dynamic. She had a quick wit and was playful. Fun. If he were in the market for a serious relationship, she was the type of woman he would be interested in. But he wasn't ready to settle down now. His career was taking off and he needed to keep his eyes on the prize—being Cowboy of the Year.

When he'd first started rodeo, people had accused him of riding on his brother's coattails. It wasn't true, but denying it hadn't changed their minds. The only way to prove them wrong was by his actions, so he'd let his victories speak for him. And they had.

Jack had worked hard to accomplish all that he had, and was making his own name. And he was only getting started. He was going to do just as well as Geoff. Then there wouldn't be a shadow of a doubt that Jack had truly made it on his own.

"So, tell me about you," Audrey said.

"What do you want to know?"

She shrugged a slender shoulder. "I don't know. We've been around each other several times in the past few days. I feel like I know some things about you, but I don't think I've gotten to know the real you. Who is Jack Burris? What makes you tick? What makes you happy? What hurts your feelings?"

"Wow, are you sure you're not a reporter?"

She inhaled audibly. "I apologize if I overstepped. I'm not trying to be nosy."

"You're not. I'm honestly not used to having deep conversations with women."

"Ah, you're more into fluff. I can do that, too. What's your favorite color? Who's your favorite singer? Do you like sports? What kind of food do you like? What's your sign?"

"I wouldn't call those questions 'fluff.' Well, maybe the one about my sign was. But wouldn't you want the person you're considering getting involved with to know what things you liked? For instance, if he wanted to surprise you with flowers, wouldn't you want him to get you the type you like? And before he bought tickets to a basketball game, wouldn't it be nice to know that you actually prefer football? And, if he wanted to surprise you by cooking dinner or taking you to a fancy restaurant, wouldn't you want it to be food that you like?

"That being said… Black or red. I don't have one. Apart from rodeo? Basketball and hockey. My mom's cooking is the best. But if I can't get that, I like Italian. And I have no idea."

She nodded slowly. "Point made. I hadn't expected such a good, well-reasoned answer." She thought for a moment. "Pink. I don't have one either. Football, but only college. And Creole. I love gumbo and jambalaya. And if you want to give me flowers, you can't go wrong with pink roses with a bit of baby's breath."

"And your sign?"

"Caution."

"That's good to know. I feel like we've just connected on a deeper level."

She laughed. He might have only been partially serious, but he did feel a certain connection to her now. Not just because he now knew her favorite color and flowers, but because it was clear that she was interested in really getting to know him. And, wonder of wonder, he wanted to know more about her.

"And as far as what makes me tick," she continued, "I like competing. And winning. There's no better feeling than doing my best and knowing that it was better than everyone else's best. There's a satisfaction that I can't describe that comes from knowing that all of my hard work has paid off," she said.

"You don't have to describe it because I know the feeling. I feel the same way."

"Of course you do."

The waitress brought their appetizer and meals to them. Neither he nor Audrey spoke until they were alone. "So tell me about your life. How did you and your sisters become involved in rodeo?"

"It's the family business. We're third-generation rodeo. My grandmother, Hattie Hawkins, was a rodeo star decades ago. She's in her seventies now, but she still has spunk and fire. Even at her age, she still rides with the best of them. When she was younger, she adopted four teenaged girls. Josie, who is my mother, Hollie, Suzie and Lisa. My mom and Hollie are Black, Suzie is white and Lisa is Latina. But they're as close as any sisters can be. And they act so much alike you would swear they shared blood. Anyway, Hattie raised them on the rodeo circuit. My mother and aunts are actually the original Hawkins Sisters. They're in their fifties now and all but retired. My sisters and I decided to use the name as an homage to them and as a way to carry on the legacy."

"Did you want to get into rodeo or was that something that was expected of you?"

"That's kind of a difficult question to answer. We were raised on the circuit, so it's something we all knew very well. In fact, the rodeo is pretty much the only life we've ever lived. To be honest, I never considered another type of life. Not that any of us were forced into it, if that's what you mean. If we wanted to do something else, our parents would have been all for it."

Jack nodded. "That's kind of the opposite of my life."

"What do you mean? All of your brothers are in rodeo."

"I know. But it's not the life my parents wanted for any of us. My mother is a kindergarten teacher and my father is a high school principal. They wanted us to go to college and get regular jobs. Safer jobs. We all participated in rodeos when we were in middle school and high school, but my parents didn't know how serious we were. They thought it was something we would all grow out of."

He bit some of his juicy ribs, chewed and swallowed before continuing. "When Geoff graduated high school, he announced that he was joining the rodeo. My parents couldn't talk him out of it, so my father traveled with him on the weekends to show him how rough it would be. But Geoff didn't change his mind. So my parents got him a good truck and wished him well."

"How did they react when you decided to join your brother? Had they mellowed?"

Laughter burst from him. "Mellowed? Not at all. One day I'll introduce you to my parents. They're wonderful, but *mellow* is not a word that describes either of them. Especially when it comes to their sons and our career choices. *Acceptance* is more like it. By the time I joined the circuit, Geoff was a huge star. He took me under his wing. We didn't compete in the same rodeos often, but when we did, it was the best."

"Was it hard to make a name for yourself? Did people treat you like Geoff's little brother and not take you seriously?"

"More times than not. How did you know?"

"Third generation. Remember? If I wasn't being compared to Brynn and always coming up short, no pun intended, then my sisters and I were being compared to our mother and aunts. Not to mention we're granddaughters of a legend. It's kind of a no-win situation."

"So how did you handle it?"

"To be honest, we're still figuring it out. You wouldn't have any tips, would you? I mean if Geoff Burris's younger brother has made a name of his own, then we should be able to step out of the shadows of the original Hawkins Sisters."

"Win more. Be better than they ever were. Make people forget their names."

He must have sounded more intense than he'd planned because she paused, her glass of cola suspended between the table and her mouth. Then she gave a slight nod, raised the glass and took a sip. He considered clarifying his remark but decided against it. After all, she was the one who'd wanted to know the real Jack Burris. And the real Jack Burris loved and admired his big brother. But he also wanted to break all of his records and make a name for himself apart from Geoff's. And that was easier said than done when his older brother had set so many records in a short time. Geoff's fame had transcended rodeo in particular and sports in general.

After a while, they switched topics, talking about the towns they'd visited over the years.

"You weren't exaggerating when you told me how good this food would be," Audrey said. She'd finished her plate of ribs and fries, cleaning every bit of meat off the bone. He hadn't believed that she would be able to eat it all. Boy, had she fooled him. As if she knew what he was thinking, she looked him in the eyes. Hers sparkled with amusement and his heart gave a strange little kick. "I have a fast metabolism."

He raised his hands in front of him. "You're in a no-judgment zone. I make no comments on what other people choose to eat. It makes no difference to me whether you eat a whole side of beef or if you only eat two crackers and an olive and call it dinner. I'm not the food police."

"You'd better knock it off, Jack."

"Knock what off?" He thought he'd been reasonable. He certainly hadn't meant to offend her.

"Being all charming. You're going to turn a girl's head."

"Would that be so bad?"

"You tell me. You're the one who decided you didn't like me after I told you who I was. I'm still Audrey Hawkins, one of the Hawkins Sisters."

He knew that. And he still didn't like the idea of women in the rodeo. He couldn't stand the idea of another woman ending up paralyzed. But he wasn't her boss. She was going to compete whether he liked it or not. Besides, they weren't competing against each other, so they could be friends.

Before he could answer, his cell beeped with a text. Audrey's phone buzzed, too. They looked at each other and smiled as they reached for their phones to read their texts.

"Is yours from Chuck Carter?" Audrey asked.

He nodded and then read the message.

Hi. I have a great idea for increasing interest in the upcoming rodeo. A Battle of the Sexes. The Burris Brothers vs the Hawkins Sisters. Sounds great, right? I think it will stir up a lot of interest. You get back to me and we'll pick events and match up competitors.

Jack put down his phone and looked at Audrey. She was smiling. No way. She couldn't possibly want to participate in something like that. It would be a circus.

"What do you think?" she asked.

"Obviously, I haven't given it much thought. But I'm leaning toward no." *Hell no* was more like it. "What do you think?"

"I think it sounds like fun. I like the idea of a family competition. People always act as if women in the rodeo are some sort of sideshow. But we aren't. We are just as talented and work just as hard as you guys do. Yet we aren't given the same respect. At least, not by everyone. And we certainly aren't given the same prize money."

"You're serious."

"Yes. Why wouldn't I be?"

"Because it's turning rodeo into a joke."

"How? Women and men have some of the same events. We rope. We ride broncs. Heck, women even ride bulls."

He knew that. But that didn't mean he agreed with it.

"You're not afraid of a little competition, are you?"

She had to be kidding. He hadn't seen the Hawkins Sisters compete, but he had no doubt that he could beat each and every one of them in competition. They might be good at what they did, but they weren't in the same league as him and his brothers. "No. Not at all."

"I'm going to tell Chuck I'm all in."

Her fingers began flying across her phone and

he reached over and captured her hand. Her skin was soft and warm, not at all what he would expect from a cowgirl. No doubt she slathered on lotion religiously. She looked at him, a question on her face. "Don't you think you should discuss this with your sisters first?"

"You're right. Brynn is always accusing me of acting before I think. And since Chuck wants all of us to compete and not just me, I shouldn't commit for all of us. Thanks. You just saved me from a major lecture from Brynn."

"You're welcome. Especially since you don't have your invisible friend to blame."

She laughed. "I never should have told you that. You're not going to let me live that down, are you?"

"I don't know. I actually think it's a sweet story. You must have been a great kid."

"I was. And I'll tell you about it one day. But I need to get going. Lunch was great. I hope we can do it again sometime."

He glanced at his watch. Wow. They had been here much longer than he'd planned. Over two hours, and yet it had felt like minutes. He couldn't recall the last time he'd had so much fun with anyone. He could get used to hanging out with her. And he wasn't sure if that was a good thing or possibly the worst thing he could do.

Chapter Five

Audrey didn't know how she'd done it, but she'd convinced Jack to let her drive his car. She wanted to think that it was because she was so charming, but it was more than likely that she'd worn down his resistance. Now as she drove along the open lane, she felt exhilarated. They were on a rural highway and going eighty miles an hour on the deserted road. Jack had let the top down and the wind whipped over them, giving her a sense of freedom that she rarely felt outside of the rodeo ring.

Jack had removed his cowboy hat and he held it in his hand. Before they'd driven over to the highway, he'd given her what could only be called a driving test. He'd explained the workings of his car in great detail, as if she'd never driven before. And she couldn't believe he'd actually asked to see her driver's license. Or that she'd actually shown it to him. But she was willing to do just about anything for the pleasure of getting behind the wheel of this car. She'd had to drive around town before he'd felt comfortable letting her on the open highway. But it had all been worth it because she was now cruising down the interstate.

She spared a glance at Jack. If she didn't know better, she'd think he looked a little bit nervous and green about the gills, as her grandmother was fond of saying. Surely, that was her imagination. He was a cowboy. He'd been on the back of bucking broncs and the rankest bulls around. He'd done some risky stunts of his own. Not to mention that he owned this car. Surely, he'd opened it up at some time if only to see what this baby could do.

But from the way he was gripping his hat with one hand and the door with the other, she would never know it. He actually looked scared. And he hadn't said a word since they'd passed a truck about twenty miles back. Of course that was only a few minutes ago. Signaling, although there was no other vehicle on the road, she slowed and then took the exit. When she reached a corner, she drove a block and turned into the deserted gas station.

She pulled into a parking spot and then turned to look at him. "That was the most fun I have had in forever. I love this car. One day I'm getting one of these."

"You certainly drove like you love it. You might not weigh much, but you have a lead foot."

She laughed. "Come on. I can't believe that you have never driven fast. This car was made for speed. Driving slowly would be an insult."

"An insult to whom?"

She looked at him and then shook her head. She'd been right. Jack didn't drive fast. Not saying he would lose a race to the stereotypical little old lady from Pasadena, but he didn't seem to appreciate what this car could do. Why would he buy a sports car if not to get from one place to another as quickly as possible?

"The designer and engineer. The people who labored to put this car together. Any number of people. Heck, me."

"You?"

"Yeah. I drive an Escape. And there's nothing wrong with that. It's reliable and serves a purpose. But I would love to have something with this horsepower. If I did? Whew. I would fly."

"And you'd spend all of your time in traffic court."

"They'd have to catch me first."

He only shook his head. "Are you ready to go back?"

She sighed. "Only if we have to."

"I suppose we could drive around a bit more before we go back to Bronco. After all, with the way you drive, it won't take more than a couple minutes to get to town."

Audrey steered the car onto the highway. She drove ten more minutes before turning around and heading for town. The car ate up the miles and before long they were back in Bronco. She slowed as she drove down the streets, taking in the quaint town as she went. From boutiques to jewelry stores to restaurants, there was just so much to like. There was something about this town—something that she couldn't quite put her finger on—that appealed to her and somehow felt familiar.

When they reached the convention center, she pulled into the parking lot and parked beside her car. She turned off the engine and looked at Jack. She couldn't decipher the expression on his face and wouldn't even try. He was much too complicated for a simple girl like her to try to understand.

"Thank you so much for today. I had a great time. Lunch was delicious and there are no words to describe how much I enjoyed driving this car."

He smiled and his brown eyes lit with pleasure, and her stomach lurched in response. He was just so sexy. "I enjoyed myself, too. Despite the hair-raising drive."

"I wasn't going that fast."

"You keep thinking that. When you passed that truck, I hollered out loud, but you were going so fast the sound couldn't keep up with us."

"I know you aren't saying we broke the sound barrier."

"I'm not, but only because I have no idea how that works."

"Neither do I, to be honest."

They sat there, grinning at each other, and Audrey knew she could be with Jack all day and night and not get bored. But she was an adult who knew that life wasn't only about having a good time. She had responsibilities, tasks that needed doing, and sitting here with Jack wasn't getting them done.

"Well, I guess I should go," she said reluctantly.

He nodded and then opened his door. She got out of the car and handed him the keys. She looked at his red car before unlocking hers. It wasn't as stylish and certainly wasn't as fast as his, but she had to remind herself that looks and speed weren't everything. As long as she could get where she needed to go and get back safely, she should be content.

Jack opened her door. "Your chariot awaits."

"Thank you."

Once she was inside, she started the engine and then rolled down the window. "I guess I'll see you around."

"You can count on it."

She nodded and then drove away, glancing into the rearview mirror. Jack stood there, watching as she drove off. Sighing, she turned and headed for the rental home.

Her sisters were waiting for her when she stepped inside.

"Don't tell me the photo shoot took that long," Brynn said.

"I could, but that would be a lie. Jack and I went out for lunch."

"Where'd you go?" Remi asked. She was sitting on the couch, reading a romance, of course. She closed the book, pulled a throw pillow up to her chest and patted the seat next to her. "Sit down and tell me all. Don't leave out a single detail."

Brynn shook her head. "I don't believe you're getting involved with him."

"Why?" Corinne asked from her place at the dining room table, where she was putting together a jigsaw puzzle. "You said not to chase him and we all agree that's good advice. But she's not chasing him. And he clearly is interested in her."

"That's true," Brynn said. She sat on a chair near the window and looked at Audrey. "Okay. Tell us everything."

"You sure did change your tune fast," Audrey said.

Brynn shrugged. "You're the only one who's dating. We might as well live vicariously through you."

"I wouldn't exactly say Jack and I are dating. We went to lunch together."

"Where did you go?" Remi asked. "See, you're already leaving out details."

Audrey blew out a breath as she sat near her sister on the sofa. "We went to DJ's Deluxe. The food is delicious, by the way. We talked, and before you ask, I'm not going to give you a blow-by-blow of the conversation."

"Phooey," Corinne said.

"Lunch was fun and we both had a great time. Afterward we went for a ride in his car. And he let me drive."

"Really? You know how men are about their cars. He must really like you," Remi said.

"And he must not know that you've never met a speed limit you didn't break, which is why I'll never ride in a car with you behind the wheel," Brynn added while Corinne nodded in agreement.

Her sisters could be wusses.

"And then he dropped me back at the convention center so I could get my car and come home."

"Did you kiss?" Remi asked.

"No." Not that she hadn't wondered about it for a second. Before her sisters could probe that statement and dissect the afternoon any more, she turned the conversation to Chuck Carter's text. "So, Chuck Carter wants us to compete in a Battle of the Sexes against the Burris brothers. What do you think?"

"He texted us, too. We were just talking about that before you walked in," Brynn said.

"I think it's a good idea," Audrey said. "When we win, we'll show the entire rodeo world that women are just as good as men."

"So you think we can win?" Corinne asked dubiously.

"Of course. Don't you?" Audrey asked. She didn't harbor the slightest doubt about her and her sisters' skills. They were second to none.

"I don't know. I really hadn't thought about it before. The competitions have always been separated by gender, which is fine by me."

"I don't think this one little competition is going to upset the status quo. It's not even about that. It's just a way to drum up more interest in the rodeo," Audrey said.

"I thought that's what all the photos and commercials were supposed to do," Remi quipped.

"This is just one more way to gain more interest," Audrey said.

Her sisters looked at each other and then back at her.

"What did you all decide?" Audrey asked.

"We hadn't reached a decision," Brynn told her.

"It sounds like fun to me," Remi said. "I'm all in."

Corinne shrugged. "I guess I'm in, too."

They looked at Brynn. "The whole idea is a little bit out there, but I'm in."

"And you know that I want to do it," Audrey said. "Let's let Chuck know what we decided. Then we just have to hope the Burris guys are as interested, too."

"What do you think?" Jack asked, looking from Ross to Mike. Ross was reclining on the sofa in their parents' family room while Jack and Mike battled on the Ping-Pong table. They had a standing tournament with Geoff and their father, Benjamin, that had been going on for as long as Jack could remember. And their father had been the undefeated champion since they'd started keeping score. Benjamin was a firm believer that as long as competitors performed their best, then no matter the outcome, they should feel good.

When they'd been little guys, barely able to see over the top of the table, he'd let them win a game or two, just to keep them from getting discouraged, and so they'd know the sweet taste of victory. Once they'd hit their teens and had started talking trash, he'd shown them no mercy. They'd soon learned the bitter taste of defeat.

"Compete against women? I don't see how that would be remotely fair to them," Ross said.

Mike picked up the Ping-Pong ball to serve. Jack held up his hand in the universal wait-a-minute sign. "I agree. I like the Hawkins sisters and the last thing I want to do is humiliate them."

"That definitely wouldn't be good for your budding romance with Audrey," Ross said.

"Let me stop you right there," Jack said, setting his paddle on the table and giving his younger brother his full attention. "There is no budding romance between me and Audrey."

"Then what about the vibe between the two of you that Willie was talking about?"

"He was just talking."

"Better not let Mom meet her or you'll end up like Geoff," Mike warned.

"Not a chance. I'm not about to propose to

anyone. But let's not get off track. I don't think we should do it either," Jack said. "What do you think, Mike?"

"I kind of like the idea."

"You would," Ross said.

"You can't be serious," Jack said. "You really want to compete against them?"

"Why not? If they're willing, I think we should be, too. After all, we don't want to look like we're afraid to go head-to-head against them."

"I hadn't thought about it that way," Ross said. "Maybe we should go ahead and do it."

"How would it work? I mean it's four of them and three of us. I have no idea if Geoff will be in town in time for the rodeo or if he would even be interested," Jack said.

"I'm sure Chuck has come up with a way to make it work," Ross said.

Jack laughed. "I wouldn't count on that. I get the feeling that he's winging it."

"Then we'll figure it out on our own," Mike said.

"So we're going to do this?" Ross asked.

Jack shrugged. "Looks like."

"All right, but don't blame us when this little competition ruins your love affair with Audrey," Ross said.

"Now you're just being annoying."

Mike picked up his paddle and ball. "Are you ready to get back to it?"

"Yep." Jack picked up his paddle as well, and they resumed the game. They were evenly matched, and the game was intense. Finally, with a last swing, Mike won.

"I let you win," Jack said.

Mike laughed. "No kidding. And here I was doing my best to let you win. But I'm just too good. Or maybe you just aren't good enough."

Ross took on the winner and the two brothers talked a lot of trash while they played. Jack tried to keep track of the points but all he could think of was Audrey and how good he felt when he was with her.

She was nothing like any woman he'd ever met before. And she certainly wasn't anything like he'd expected her to be. He was going to have to toss aside all of his preconceived notions and get to know her over time. He smiled as he recalled the way she'd driven his car. She was daring and had been in complete control, enjoying the power of the engine and the easy speed it produced.

Jack had been looking forward to spending more time with her. But if they were going to compete against each other, he would have to reconsider that idea. Competitors could be friendly, but they couldn't be friends. Not when there was only one prize. Of course, his brothers were the exception to that rule. If he didn't win the night, he always hoped that one of them would.

However, that didn't solve his problem with Audrey. They weren't related by blood. And though he'd denied it, he was attracted to her. She could easily become a distraction, keeping him from competing at his highest level. He hoped that she and her sisters decided not to compete in the Battle of the Sexes. That would make things so much easier. But judging from the excitement on her face when she'd read the text, he had a sneaking suspicion that wasn't going to be the case.

So what was he going to do now?

Chapter Six

Jack poured coffee into his cup and sat at the kitchen table the next morning. He, Ross and Mike had gone on an early morning five-mile run. When they'd gotten home, a note was taped to the refrigerator. *Went to Zumba so you're on your own for breakfast. Do not leave a mess in my kitchen. Love, Mom.*

They'd rock-paper-scissored over who would have to take the last shower and who would have to cook breakfast. When they'd been teenagers, their father had added a bathroom in the base-ment, which was the shower Jack had ended up using. Mike had lost out and was now in the upstairs shower while Jack and Ross were in the kitchen cooking breakfast.

"I think he lost on purpose so he doesn't have to help cook," Ross said, stirring the grits. He'd already made toast and Jack had scrambled eggs and put a tray of turkey bacon in the oven.

"He'd better hurry up or he's going to be eating cold food because I'm not waiting on him."

"I'm here now," Mike said, stepping into the room. "And eating cold food has never bothered me."

"Good. I hope washing the dishes doesn't bother you, either, because Mom won't be happy coming home to a dirty kitchen," Ross said, setting his plate on the table and then sitting down.

Mike grinned as he fixed his plate. "But she won't be mad at me. I'm the baby."

Jack and Ross groaned. Although he was twenty-four, Mike had learned early on that playing the baby card could get him out of more than a few lectures. Of course, the older brothers knew that, too, and often used Mike as the front man to get them out of trouble when one of their hijinks had landed them in hot water.

"But I'm her favorite," Ross and Jack said in unison. That was the family joke. Their mother had always made each of her sons feel as if he were her favorite.

"Keep telling yourselves that."

The brothers joked and kidded each other while they ate. They were putting their plates in the dishwasher when Jack's phone rang. It was Willie, the photographer. "What's up, Willie?"

Jack put the phone on speaker so that he could continue to help clean the kitchen.

"The proofs are ready for you and Audrey to come look at. Of course, Chuck and the organizers will make the decision about which to use for the promotion, but I'll let you each have one or two pictures provided you don't share them with anyone."

"That sounds good," Jack said. His brothers had stopped working and were now staring at him. He should have known better than to put his phone on speaker. But they were a part of the promotion, too, so they had a right to know what was going on.

"I already called Audrey to let her know. She's agreed to come in around noon. Does that work for you?"

"Yep." Jack ended the call and then leaned against the counter and looked at his brothers. "Go ahead and get it out of your systems."

"What do you mean?" Ross asked in fake innocence.

"Whatever you're going to say about me and Audrey and our pictures."

"You already said that there's nothing going on, so what's there to say?"

"Yeah, besides you managed to take all of the fun out of it," Mike added.

Jack laughed. They finished cleaning the kitchen and he headed to his room. When he was alone, he called Audrey. His heart began pounding in his chest as he thought about seeing her again, which was ridiculous. He wasn't some fifteen-year-old calling to ask his crush to go to the movies with him.

She answered on the second ring.

"Hey, Jack. I take it that Willie has called you."

"Yeah. We just hung up. If you want, I can pick you up and we can go together."

"Are you going to let me drive?"

"I suppose so. After all, we'll be in town the entire time, so there's no risk of you going warp speed."

She giggled and the sound did strange things to his stomach. This was getting out of control. He liked Audrey. There was no secret to that. But the way his body was reacting, you'd think there was something more than friendship between them.

"Then I'd love to go with you."

"I'll pick you up about eleven thirty."

"I'll be waiting."

It isn't a date.
Well, it isn't exactly hanging out with a friend.
If that was the case, she'd have showered,

pulled her hair into a ponytail on top of her head, and put on her favorite jeans and T-shirt and called it a day.

Instead she'd put on makeup, curled her hair and tried on several outfits before deciding on a pink floral top that accentuated her curves and a pink denim skirt and white sandals. She'd added some rarely worn earrings, a necklace and several bangles to complete the look. She was nearly to the door when she paused and returned to her dresser. She grabbed the bottle of her favorite perfume, sprayed it into the air and stepped into the mist. Now she was ready to go.

Remi was sitting on the couch when Audrey entered the room.

"You look nice," Remi said, looking up from her book.

"Thanks. Jack and I are going to check out the pictures that Willie took of us yesterday."

"Really? Two dates in two days."

"It's not a date. We're just going to check out the proofs. And since we both want to see them, it only makes sense to go together."

Remi held her hands out in front of her as if in surrender. "Hey, you don't have to justify anything to me. If you recall, I'm the sister who's all for you and Jack dating. I think you make a cute couple. Besides, the two of you have chemistry."

"Right," Audrey said, trying to keep her voice even.

As much as she wanted to deny that there was something between her and Jack, or at least nothing that was visible to others, she had to admit that he made her feel emotions she hadn't felt in quite a while. It was hard to maintain a committed relationship when she wasn't in one place very long. Most men weren't interested in having a long-distance relationship with someone who was always on the road.

And then there were the cowboys. They traveled as much as she did and understood the lifestyle and commitment it took to excel. She'd dated a cowboy once briefly and it hadn't turned out well. They'd spent more time apart than they had together. Neither of them had been willing to sacrifice their career in favor of their relationship. There hadn't been a big, messy breakup. Or a breakup at all. In the end, the relationship had just sort of faded away.

But even without hurtful words or anger between them, the experience had left a mark on Audrey and she was determined not to make the same mistake again. Rodeo and relationships didn't mix. Especially with a cowboy.

Not that she was under the impression that Jack wanted to have a relationship with her. He hadn't done anything to give her that notion, despite the fact that her overly romantic sister wanted to believe there was a romance brewing between them.

"I'm serious. You and Jack have chemistry. And that's the most important ingredient that you need in a romance."

"Okay. On that note, I think I'll wait for Jack on the porch." The romance Remi was spinning was starting to sound good and Audrey needed to get away before she got swept up in it.

"Hey," Remi called as Audrey opened the front door.

"Yeah?"

"Willie didn't call the rest of us. Are there any proofs of the pictures we all took together?"

"To be honest, I don't know. He only mentioned the pictures that Jack and I took together. But I'll ask him about the rest."

"Thanks. It would be cool to see them, but it's not a big deal."

"I'll ask," Audrey repeated and then went outside and sat on the porch swing.

It was a beautiful day. The sun was shining brightly in the clear blue sky and there was a slight breeze. Perfect weather for an August day. She inhaled the fresh air and then pushed against the floor, setting the swing in motion.

Two kids on bikes rode past the Colonial while three girls jumped rope in front of the house next door. This was a family neighborhood. There were plenty of young couples with small children as well as older people with grandchildren who frequently came to visit. Although Audrey and her sisters hadn't lived here for long, there was something about this block that felt familiar, which didn't make a lot of sense. She'd never lived anyplace remotely like Bronco.

She spotted Jack's car as he drove down the street and she stood as he pulled in front of her house. He hopped out of the car and was up the stairs in the blink of an eye. She couldn't help but stare. He was dressed in dark jeans and a nice shirt. As usual, he was wearing boots and a winner's buckle on his hand-tooled belt. And, of course, he had on his black cowboy hat. All in all, he looked good enough to eat.

"Hi," she said. Her voice sounded strangely breathless and she cleared her throat and tried again. "How are you?"

"Great. How are you?"

"I'm excited to see these pictures."

He grinned. "So am I. To hear Willie tell it,

he's taken the photographic equivalent of the *Mona Lisa*."

"As long as we don't end up looking like the couple in that *American Gothic* painting."

Jack laughed. "No way that happens. You're much too cute."

"Thank you."

He nodded and then they walked down the stairs to his car, where he opened the driver's door for her and then stepped aside so she could get in.

"I can't believe you're letting me drive."

"Why? I told you that I would. My parents raised me to keep my word."

"I know. But you didn't have to say yes in the first place."

"No worries. Besides, we're not going very far."

"So we won't be taking the highway?"

"Sorry, but no."

"No matter. This is probably better."

"Better? Why?"

"Because everyone in town will be able to see me driving this really sexy car. They'll think I'm cool."

"Not everyone in town."

"Well, everyone we pass. My neighbors will be impressed anyway." They passed two teenaged boys who watched as they drove by. The boys smiled and nodded in admiration. "Told you."

"So your goal is to impress teenaged boys."

"I take my fans wherever I can find them."
Jack nodded.

"So where are we going? I have the address
but I'm not sure of the directions."

"Do you remember where DJ's Deluxe is?"

"Yep. My stomach will never forget. Best ribs
I've had in a long time."

"It's only a couple of blocks from there."

"Okay. I think I can get there."

"How do you like this neighborhood?" Jack
asked as she drove down the street.

"I love it. It's a real family community. The
neighbors are nice, too."

"I know. My parents live not too far from here."

"Really? How close?"

"About half a mile away."

"You and your brothers are staying with them,
right?"

"Yes. As always. My mother loves having us
around. My father does, too, although he says he
doesn't like sharing his best girl with us."

"Oh, how sweet. Your parents sound so cute."

"They are." He paused and she felt him looking over at her. "What are your parents like?"

"Separated at the moment."

"Oh. Sorry."

"Don't be. I believe my parents love each other
and that this is a temporary thing. But if not, it's

their choice. They have to do what makes them happy."

"I agree. And what makes you happy?"

"Rodeo. Being with my sisters." And spending time with him, but she wasn't going to say that. That was just a bit too forward and revealing.

They arrived at the studio right then and she parked. They entered the stately brick building and went to the second floor. A plaque advertising Picture This Photography Studio was beside an oak door. They knocked and then stepped into a small reception area. A navy love seat was flanked by two navy chairs. The room had floor-to-ceiling windows and was flooded with light.

"Right on time," Willie said as he stepped into the reception area. He extended his hand to them. After shaking hands, he gestured behind him. "Come on back into my conference room. I have the pictures all laid out for you."

His conference room turned out to be a slightly larger room. Instead of a desk, there was an enormous table in the center of the room with four chairs pushed against the walls. As with the reception area, this room was also well lit. Dozens of photographs were piled on the table. Willie shoved a few aside and then looked up at them, his ever-present smile even brighter than usual.

"Wait until you see these," he said. He picked up a four-by-six photograph, handed it to her and then stood back, clearly expecting her to be impressed.

Even if she hadn't been, there was no way she would say it out loud. He was so eager that disappointing him would be like hurting a puppy.

She glanced at the picture and her mouth fell open. "Oh, my goodness. This is wonderful."

"I told you it would be."

The photograph was one of the candid shots Willie had taken when Audrey and Jack had been talking before the start of the photo shoot. They were looking at each other, their eyes filled with emotion. Their bodies seemed to be leaning toward each other. No, that wasn't quite right. It was as if some invisible force was pulling them together. Like two magnets being drawn together. The connection between them was palpable.

She could also sense the longing between them. It was as if each of them had found something they'd been searching for in the other. She shook her head. That was fanciful even for her. She was reading way too much into a simple photograph.

"Let me see," Jack said. Audrey was suddenly aware of how near he was to her. Of the heat radiating from his body and wrapping around her, as if encouraging her to feel things for him that she wasn't sure she wanted to feel.

She handed over the photograph. Their hands brushed and she felt an electrical shock from the contact. He must have felt it, too, because his eyes shot to hers. They were darker and filled with an intensity that hadn't been there previously. She released the picture and took a step away from him, needing to create physical distance. Hopefully emotional distance would follow. She grabbed a random photograph from the table, hoping to make her movement less obvious.

"What do you think?" Willie asked Jack.

Audrey glanced at Jack out of the corner of her eye. She needed to see if he'd been as affected by the picture as she'd been.

"It's...good."

Good? That was all he had? Perhaps she had seen more than what had actually been there. It was only a picture, for goodness' sake.

"It's..." Jack seemed lost for words.

"Revealing?" Willie supplied.

"You definitely caught us unaware."

"Yes. A good photographer is able to peel away the masks and capture the essence of his subjects. He's able to reveal the real feelings, even if the people are trying to hide them. Or perhaps are completely unaware of them." Willie looked at them meaningfully.

Jack nodded. "I see what you mean."

"Have a look at some more," Willie said. "I've set out the best ones for you to look at. And don't forget, I can make copies of a few of them for you.

Pull up a chair and sit while you review them. I've got a few things to do, so I'll be in my office. Holler if you need anything."

Audrey and Jack grabbed chairs and then sat at the table. After looking at a couple of the pictures in silence, Jack covered her hand with his. She looked at their joined hands and then up to his face. His eyes were dark and mysterious.

"What do you think?" He showed her the picture Willie had taken where Jack had Audrey draped over his shoulder. They'd both been laughing, and their smiles were bright. Audrey liked that picture much better than the one that had revealed her secret feelings.

"I think that I should have pulled on your belt and given you a wedgie."

Jack roared with laughter. "I mean about the picture."

She took a closer look. "Willie definitely has a gift. Just looking at it brings back how much fun we had that day."

"It was fun."

"Do you think other people will be able to pick up on that from looking at the picture? Or do you think we feel more because these pictures bring back memories for us?"

"I think other people will know that we were having fun. They'll be able to pick up on our feelings."

Just what she was afraid of. After only looking at a handful of pictures, it was obvious that she was attracted to Jack. It was bad enough that her sisters knew. Audrey didn't want the entire world to know what she was still coming to grips with. A girl needed some privacy.

They looked at a few dozen photos. When they'd seen them all, they called Willie back into the room.

He looked at Audrey and Jack, a pleased expression on his face. "These tell quite the story, don't you think?"

Audrey agreed. Too bad it was a story she wanted to keep untold.

"Do you want a copy of any?"

Jack picked up the photo of him with Audrey slung over his shoulder. She shook her head. "You would choose that one."

"I like it. It looks like I'm winning even though we both know that I didn't."

"How do you figure that?"

He pointed at a picture they'd taken where she'd been standing on the bleacher with him beside her. Audrey frowned. Of all of the pictures they'd taken together, the posed ones were her least favorite. They seemed stiff and lacking emotion. She much preferred the candid ones. "We're by the bleachers."

"Which one do you want?" Willie asked Audrey.

She picked up the first picture Willie had shown them. There was something about the emotion there that she couldn't deny. But would she be giving away too much if she asked for a copy? Especially since Jack was currently looking at her. Well, too bad. It was the picture she wanted.

"Give me a minute," Willie said. "Believe it or not, you've chosen two of my favorites. But then, just about all of them are my favorite."

Willie excused himself and then disappeared once more, leaving Audrey and Jack alone. Audrey was trying to think of something to say to fill the silence. Odd that she was struggling with that when up until this moment conversation had come easily.

Before she could come up with a topic, Willie was back. He handed them each an envelope and they stood.

"I'll get the rest of the proofs to Chuck. From here on out, everything is out of my hands. He'll select the pictures he wants to use for the campaign."

"Thanks," Jack said.

"Speaking of the campaign, do you know when you'll have the rest of the pictures ready? One of my sisters asked me about them and I told her I'd check with you."

"I should have those together by the end of the week."

"Thanks." Audrey shook his hand. "I really appreciate getting a sneak peek at these."

"It was my pleasure. It's not often that I come across such a dynamic couple with such an interesting story to tell."

Jack and Audrey left then.

"What did you and your brothers decide about the Battle of the Sexes?" Audrey asked as they walked back to Jack's car.

"We decided to do it."

"Really?"

"Well, Ross and Mike and I. Geoff is off fulfilling other commitments, and we don't know if he'll be around. None of us felt like we should agree to something on his behalf. Chuck was good with just the three of us competing. That is, if you and your sisters agreed to compete."

Jack's voice sounded strained and Audrey stopped walking and looked at him. He was holding his body stiffly as he awaited her answer, and she couldn't determine whether he was hoping she'd say yes or hoping she'd say no. Well, there was only one way to find out. "We're going to compete. Brynn should have called Chuck by now to let him know."

"So, the Battle of the Sexes is a go."

"Yep. The Hawkins Sisters versus the Burris Brothers. May the best team win."

Chapter Seven

Jack heard Audrey's words and it was all he could do not to frown. He didn't want to battle it out with Audrey and her sisters. Being with her was the most fun he'd had in a long time. But if they were going to compete against each other, they couldn't hang out.

Even though the Battle of the Sexes was simply a way of bringing more people out to see the rodeo, he still intended to do his best as he always did. The people who were buying tickets to the exhibition deserved to see a good show.

That meant he couldn't allow himself to be distracted. And Audrey Hawkins was nothing if not distracting.

The more time he spent with her, the more time he wanted to spend with her. It was as if he'd become addicted to her presence. Heck, he'd dreamed of her last night, something that had never happened before. It had been so real that he'd reached out for her as he'd awakened this morning, expecting her to be beside him. When his cold sheets had been the only thing he'd encountered, he'd felt cheated. Clearly, she was taking over his life, and calling her a distraction was an understatement.

There was only one thing he could do. Until the rodeo was over, he was going to have to keep her at a distance. No more lunches together. No more letting her drive his car. No more hanging out together just because it was fun. He needed to focus, and that was something he wasn't capable of doing when Audrey was around.

"So, how are we going to divide the events so that it's fair?" Audrey asked, breaking into his thoughts.

"What do you mean?"

"It's four of us and only three of you. Somebody is going to have to compete more than once."

"That won't be a problem. Each of us is capable of competing in any event. Ross and I each ride bulls on the circuit, and Mike has been known to do it on occasion, although it's not his favorite event. All three of us bronc ride. We all rope and ride and know how to barrel race. The question is more for you and your sisters anyway."

She frowned and he wondered what he'd said to upset her. Clearly, he'd said something wrong.

"We are expert on every event, so don't worry about us holding up our end."

"I wasn't." Great. This stupid Battle of the Sexes hadn't even started and it was already causing problems between them. Stress was the last thing he needed. Because even though the battle between the two families was a side event, the rodeo was real, and he intended to win the events in the actual rodeo.

She didn't seem mollified, but she did stop frowning at him. "How about lunch? I had an early breakfast and I'm hungry."

"Okay." Hadn't he just decided that he needed to keep his distance from her? Yes. And he intended to let her know. But there was no reason he had to do it on an empty stomach. "How about pizza?"

"Sounds good. Can I drive?"

"You know, I'm starting to think you only like me for my car."

She grinned at him. "Nah. I'm hanging around you because you're great arm candy. I attract all kinds of attention whenever you're around."

He laughed. She was hilarious and seemed to

know just what to say to defuse a tense situation. But then, she didn't know that he was ending things between them. She probably wouldn't be making jokes if she did.

"I'm not sure that's the reason you're getting so much attention, but you just might be right." He preened and then tipped his cowboy hat at her.

"So are you going to let me drive or not?"

"Absolutely. Only a fool would blow the opportunity to have such an attractive chauffeur."

"Call me what you want, just hand over the keys."

They joked and laughed the short distance to the pizza joint and again all throughout lunch. It wouldn't be an exaggeration to say he was having the time of his life.

As they ate, they told tales of their adventures on the rodeo. Her eyes grew dark with intensity as she recounted an adventure in barrel racing. He could picture her astride her horse as she flew around the barrels in an effort to erase seconds from her time. She was definitely a dynamo.

After they'd finished their lunches, they lingered at the table. The ice had melted in their sodas, but neither of them made a move to leave.

"Hey, aren't you Jack Burris?"

Jack turned and found himself face-to-face with a young boy. "Yes, I am."

"Me and my dad saw you in the Mistletoe Rodeo last year, didn't we, Dad?"

The man standing beside him nodded.

"You were really good."

"Thanks."

"There's going to be another rodeo," the kid said. "Are you going to be in it?"

"I am. As a matter of fact, we both are," Jack said, nodding at Audrey. "We'll even be competing against each other."

"But she's a girl," the kid said. Clearly confused, he rubbed a finger under his nose.

"Yes, she is."

"You can't compete against a girl. You're bigger than she is."

"True," Jack agreed.

The kid sighed dramatically. "So I guess you're going to have to let her win or she'll start crying."

"I'm not going to cry if I don't win," Audrey said. "I hope Jack won't cry when I beat him."

"You won't beat him," the kid said. "Girls can't beat boys at sports."

"On that note, I think we'll be leaving," the kid's father said, giving them an apologetic look. "It was nice meeting you both. Enjoy the rest of your day."

Jack watched as the man hustled the little boy away from his table.

"Well, that was…interesting," Audrey said.

Jack didn't even pretend to know how he was

supposed to respond. He did know that whatever he said would no doubt be the wrong thing. "Um," he settled for saying. That was neutral and not likely to get him into trouble.

"Little chauvinist in training."

"Oh, come on, Audrey. He's a kid. Maybe he has a little sister who cries when she loses games, so he thinks all girls are the same. Not that you're a girl," he hastened to add.

Audrey gave him a skeptical look.

He sighed. "The fact is women and men compete separately in rodeo. Heck, in sports in general."

"Perhaps we compete separately for reasons that have nothing to do with our abilities. And look at the result. Little boys automatically thinking that women aren't able to beat men unless the man lets it happen. And of course he has to let her win or the emotional woman will burst into tears."

"Audrey, let it go. That was one little boy. He couldn't be more than six. Obviously he hasn't had many life experiences."

Audrey huffed out a breath. "Sorry. I just get upset when people assume that women in rodeo aren't as good as men. We work hard to perfect our skills, the same as you do."

"I know. And speaking of perfecting our skills, I won't be able to spend as much time with you as I have been. I need to concentrate on getting ready for the competition."

"I see."

"It's the professional thing to do." At least, that was the excuse he was going with. It sounded reasonable. The truth was he'd seen the candid pictures Willie had snapped. The expression on his face had been revealing. Too revealing. He'd been looking at Audrey like she was the best thing he'd ever seen. The raw emotion on his face scared him. And it was more than he wanted to deal with right now. He needed to put some distance between them before his feelings got the better of him. But he couldn't tell her that. He had no idea how she would interpret that and he didn't want to find out.

"Is it?" Her voice was chillier than he had ever heard it and the sparkle that he had grown accustomed to seeing in her eyes was gone. Now they were just as cold as her voice. In fact, there was no warmth to be found anywhere. She was just as icy as a December Montana night.

Obviously, he had said something wrong. He mentally replayed his words. When he couldn't find the mistake, he decided he must not have expressed himself clearly. "Yes. I want to be at my best and I'm sure you do, too. Because we don't only have the competition between our families to think about, we need to focus on the real events."

"And the ones between us aren't real?"

"You know what I mean. The events that count toward point totals. The ones that make or break a year. You heard how Chuck described the competitions between us. They're exhibitions meant to draw in the casual fan."

"A sideshow."

He had a feeling that he was stepping into a trap, but since it was the way he felt, he replied honestly.

"Exactly."

She glared at him and then jerked around, pulling her purse into her lap. She opened it and yanked out her wallet. Giving him a death stare, she pulled out several bills and handed them to him.

"What's this?"

"You paid for my lunch."

"I know."

"Well, I don't want you to do that. I can pay my own way. And I want to make one thing perfectly clear, Jack Burris."

First and last name. That was ominous, and only meant one thing. Trouble was on the way and it had his name written all over it. "What's that?"

"I'm going to wipe up the floor with you. I'm going to beat you so bad in every event that you're going to be the one in tears."

That said, she jumped up from her chair and strode angrily from the restaurant. Jack stared after her and then added the bills to the tip he'd left for the waitress. He stood and patted his pocket. Great, she had his car keys. He hoped she hadn't left him stranded. If he had to call one of his brothers for a ride, he'd never hear the end of it.

Making a big dramatic exit only worked when you could actually leave. Audrey stood outside the entrance of the pizza joint, clutching Jack's keys in her hands. Great. Well, there was absolutely no way she was going to walk back into that place. Not after making her pronouncement.

There was a lesson in this. Next time, she was driving her own car.

No matter how badly she wanted to leave, she couldn't drive away in his car. That would be tantamount to stealing. Despite how petty it was, she smiled as she pictured him coming out of the door only to discover his car was gone. She could just imagine the outraged expression on his face.

A group of teenaged boys approached the door and she stepped aside so they could enter. She glanced at her watch, wishing Jack would hurry up. She didn't like the idea of loitering out here. It made her look like she'd been stood up.

"Hey, if your guy doesn't show, you can always join us," one of the teenagers said.

"Thanks, but I'm fine."

"Yes, you are," another one of them said, and she rolled her eyes. These boys weren't old enough to shave and had probably been dropped off by one of their mothers.

"She has a date," Jack said, pushing through the teens. Their bravado fell away as they looked at him.

"Thanks anyway, guys," she said.

"Sure." They went into the pizza parlor, her and Jack forgotten.

Audrey narrowed her eyes and looked at Jack. "Let's get something straight. You aren't my date."

"Maybe not, but I am your ride home."

She dangled his car keys in front of him. "Actually, I'm your ride home."

He shook his head and then held out his hands. "I should probably drive back."

"Why? You don't trust me all of a sudden?"

He blew out a breath and dropped his hand. "You can drive."

She walked beside him to his car and got in. The ride to her house was quiet and tense, completely different than the other times they'd ridden together. They didn't say more than two words to each other. When she got back to her house, she turned off the ignition and then looked at him. "I meant what I said earlier, Jack. I'm going to beat you in every event we have."

He held out his hand to shake. "May the best man win."

She slapped his hand away. "Cute. In this instance, the best man is going to be a woman."

She stormed into the house, the envelope with her picture beneath her arm. Fortunately, none of her sisters was around and she made it to her room without having to talk to anyone.

Remi and Corinne had been so enthusiastic about her developing a relationship with Jack, and for a moment, she'd been carried away by the idea. Brynn had been right. She should have kept her distance from Jack until she'd discovered his true character. Of course, even after the time she'd spent with him, she still wasn't sure what his true character was.

Sometimes he could be so considerate, making her feel that she was important to him. It was a small thing, but she liked the way he always held open the door for her, the way he pulled out her chair. He was so gallant. And she loved his sense of humor and the way he appreciated hers. He got her jokes. They laughed at the same things. Heck, he often said something mere moments before the exact words came out of her mouth.

There was no question that they had a lot in common. And all things being even, that might be enough. But for all of his good qualities, he had one major flaw. He didn't think cowgirls were equal to cowboys.

He actually regarded the Battle of the Sexes as a sideshow. As if the whole competition was some type of carnival act. Well, she would show him. And her sisters would show his brothers. The Hawkins Sisters were going to do something no other cowgirls had ever done. They were going to beat the men in a head-to-head event.

Her anger fueled her until she glanced at the envelope Willie had given her. Then it burned out. She wanted to look at the picture inside, but she knew doing so would only cause her to weaken. She couldn't look at the emotions she and Jack had on their faces without feeling what she'd felt in those moments. The dozens of photos had told a story. And from all indications, the story was a romance.

But that was ridiculous. Maybe she was misinterpreting the pictures. Perhaps it was only desire that she saw. And that would make perfect sense because Jack was a gorgeous man. He was one-hundred-percent grade A. His clear brown skin, mischievous smile, complete with white teeth and a dimple, and intelligent eyes were the stuff of a woman's dream. She found herself drooling at the memory of how good his thighs looked in his jeans.

So perhaps simple lust was the reason why he was always on her mind and it had nothing to do with her heart.

She knew she was lying to herself, but for now, it would have to do.

Chapter Eight

A few days later, Audrey and her sisters met at the convention center to learn more about the promotion for the Bronco Summer Family Rodeo and the Battle of the Sexes. As expected, Jack and his brothers were there. Audrey hadn't seen or spoken to him since the day they'd had their big fight, and as much as she hated to admit it, she was hungry for a look at him. And he didn't disappoint.

Dressed in black jeans, a white shirt and his cowboy hat, he looked better than she remembered. There was something so electric about him. He always seemed to radiate energy. Even when he'd been standing still, he seemed ready to spring into action. Regardless, when she saw him, she merely nodded politely and then sat in one of the seats arranged in a semicircle in a corner of the arena.

She glanced over at Corinne, who was talking to Mike. She couldn't hear what he was saying, but whatever it was had her sister grinning from ear to ear. Corinne put a hand on Mike's shoulder and then they both laughed. *Oh, no. Please don't tell me that Corinne and Mike are starting a thing.*

Not that she had anything against Mike. He seemed friendly and easygoing. That day of the photo shoot, there had been lots of teasing, often with Mike being targeted by his brothers. He'd taken it all in stride, laughing at himself. And Audrey loved Corinne. She wanted nothing more than for her sister to have a relationship with a man who appreciated her and who wanted to make her happy.

But why did that person have to be Jack Burris's younger brother? Seeing them crush on each other was the last thing she needed right now, especially since things with Jack had gone kaput so quickly.

Chuck Carter and his assistant, Katy, entered the arena. They were carrying easels and several large poster boards. Realizing the meeting was about to begin, the rest of the group quickly took seats. Remi took the empty chair next to Ross. That left the only seat for Jack next to Audrey. Remi smirked and Audrey glared in return.

Jack sat by Audrey and immediately she was engaged in a struggle to keep control of herself. The part of her that was still foolishly attracted to him wanted to lean over and breathe in his scent. The part of her that knew better had her sitting up so straight in the folding chair that it was a wonder her back didn't crack. The chairs were so close together that his shoulder brushed against hers. The cotton of his shirt felt soft against her bare arm. Goose bumps popped up on her flesh and she was irrationally angry at him for her reaction.

Chuck stood in front of the group. "Thanks for coming. I just wanted to let you see what we've come up with to promote the Bronco Summer Family Rodeo since your families are the highlight of the event." He set the first poster on the easel and then stepped aside so everyone could take a look.

Despite being incredibly aware of every move Jack made, Audrey was struck by the image in front of her and she couldn't hold back a smile. It was one of the pictures Willie had taken with the two families standing back-to-back, holding lassos in their hands. The words "It's on" were written in red letters beneath the photo.

Chuck removed that poster board and replaced it with another one. This time, they were facing each other. Willie had told them to look fierce. Naturally, they had all burst into laughter. Eventually they had all managed to have fierce expressions on their faces at the same time. Instead of that pose, though, Chuck had selected one of them laughing. The words "Fun for the whole family, even competitors" were written below in bold letters.

Audrey looked at the poster more closely, taking in every detail. She and Jack had been across from each other. Their gazes were locked, and their mutual attraction was on full display. She crossed her fingers and hoped the others were so busy looking at the picture in its entirety that they didn't notice the connection between her and Jack.

Chuck showed two more posters, each one playing up the family angle. Audrey had to give the man credit. The ad campaign he'd put together made the rodeo very appealing. If she wasn't a participant, she would be on the phone right now ordering tickets.

"What do you think?" Chuck asked.

"You've done a wonderful job," Brynn said, and everyone quickly echoed that sentiment.

"I'm glad you like it. I'm convinced having two of rodeo's most famous families will be a selling point for parents, especially those with daughters. Little girls will see the Hawkins Sisters as role models. But there's another segment of the public that we want to draw in as well. And that's older teens and people in their twenties. The Battle of the Sexes is designed to bring them in. These next posters play up that angle."

He set the next poster on the easel. There was a collective gasp and then Audrey felt everyone's eyes turn to look at her.

"Wowza," Remi said, rising and going to the easel to get a closer look. In a blink, Audrey's two other sisters and Jack's brothers were on their feet, gathered around the easel. They were talking over each other, so it was hard for Audrey to make out more than "hot," "sexy" and other words she'd prefer not to acknowledge.

Audrey couldn't tear her eyes away from the poster, even though it was hard to see much with the people blocking her view. But she didn't need to see it. The image of her and Jack smiling at each other was seared into her mind. Chuck had chosen to use the photo of her and Jack being pulled toward each other. They weren't standing especially close, but there was an unmistakable intimacy between them that she couldn't deny. No matter how much she wished it were otherwise, she and Jack shared a connection. She didn't know how it had been created, so she had no idea how to break it.

When everyone had gotten their fill of admiring the picture, they returned to their seats. Chuck revealed four other posters featuring her and Jack, and each one received the same reaction. The posters told a compelling story, drawing in the viewer. The text had been sparse, letting the photographs do the talking.

The last poster had headshots of her and Jack with the words "Who will end up on top?" written beneath them.

"That is some top-notch advertising," Ross said. "I'm interested to see how this Battle of the Sexes turns out myself." He looked at the Hawkins sisters, his eyes twinkling with mischief. "Who am I up against?"

"I'll take you on," Brynn said instantly. "Just name the event."

"How are we going to make it work with odd numbers?" Corinne asked. "I'm willing to sit it out, if necessary."

"That won't be necessary," Chuck said. "Unless there's an event you don't ordinarily compete in, you'll each compete in all of the events and we'll average the scores. As far as the team roping events go, you can mix and match as you choose."

"That sounds fair," Remi said.

"And, of course, we'll have the individual battle between Audrey and Jack to start things off."

"The what?" Jack said. "I thought this was a family versus family deal. Nobody ever said anything about me and Audrey having a separate battle."

"Yeah, I know. I came up with this idea after seeing the pictures of the two of you together. There's something there and we need to capitalize on it."

"I don't know," Jack said slowly.

"You aren't scared, are you?" Mike asked with a chuckle.

"Yeah, you aren't scared, are you, Jack?" Audrey said. Unlike Mike, she was serious.

"Not at all," Jack replied flatly, a challenge in his eyes.

"Then it's all settled," Chuck said, rubbing his hands together. "This is going to be so great."

Audrey glanced over at Jack, hating the tension between them. *Yeah. Just great.*

"So what's going on between you and Audrey?" Ross asked Jack that evening after dinner. Their parents had gone for a walk around the neighborhood and Jack and Ross were sitting on the porch. "Trouble in paradise?"

"I have no idea what you're talking about."

"It's me you're talking to. So don't pretend that

there's not some romance or whatever going on."
He looked Jack in the eyes. "You can tell me.
Brothers don't blab. You know that."

Jack knew. He and his brothers had been keeping each other's secrets all of their lives. It wasn't
as if he didn't trust Ross. It was just that he didn't
have the words to describe what he felt for Audrey. His feelings for her ran the gamut, changing by the hour and with each interaction. One
minute, she had him laughing so hard his sides
ached. The next, he was so angry he felt steam
rising from his head.

Nevertheless, that wasn't the problem. The
problem was he wanted to touch her. Kiss her.
Hold her in his arms. But now they were competing against each other. The family competition
was bad enough. A head-to-head battle was ten
times worse. It wouldn't be so hard if he wasn't
developing feelings for her and if he couldn't tell
she had feelings for him. Then it would all be in
good fun with nothing to lose. But that wasn't
the case.

"Nothing to tell. We had been spending time
together, but now that the rodeo is getting close,
I need to focus on that. I told her as much, but
she took it as an insult."

"So you put her on the shelf."

"No. I just told her that I need to step back.

She's a professional, so she knows what I mean. She's a competitor herself, so she knows what it takes to be at your best."

"Well, that explains it."

"Explains what?"

"Her Instagram post about you."

"About me?"

Ross handed over his phone. "See for yourself."

Jack took his brother's phone and then looked at the post. It was a picture of Audrey next to her horse. Before he looked at the text, he took a minute to study her. She looked absolutely gorgeous in her red blouse with white fringe and white cowboy hat. He almost reached out and caressed her cheek but stopped himself just in time. He didn't want Ross to know just how drawn he was to Audrey. But then, Ross had seen the pictures of the two of them, so he would already know how Jack felt. Every person who looked at those posters would know.

Jack read the message beneath the image.

Hey, friends. Are you up for a #BattleOfTheSexes? Come on down to the Bronco Summer Family Rodeo and watch me show Jack Burris what a woman can do. People say may the best man win, but that's only when a woman isn't around. Jack Burris will be coming in second place. You can bet on it.

Oh, no, she didn't. Jack pulled out his phone.

"Think before you respond," Ross cautioned him.

Jack glared at his brother. "If she didn't want the smoke, she shouldn't have started the fire."

Ross raised his hands. "When you lose the girl, don't say I didn't warn you."

That comment wasn't worthy of a reply so Jack didn't give him one. Instead, he wrote beneath Audrey's post.

Make no mistake about it, the best MAN is going to win.

"Satisfied?" Ross asked.

"Not even close. It's time to make a post of my own."

He scrolled through his saved photos until he found one of him on the back of a bull. It was his first ninety-point ride, and the winning score of the rodeo. The event photographer had caught him midspin while the bull leapt in the air. This had always been his favorite picture. Or at least it had been until he'd seen the ones he'd taken with Audrey.

He posted that photo to his Instagram with a comment.

Let's see you beat this, Audrey Hawkins.

A moment later a comment appeared on his post.

Not to worry. You'll have a front-row seat.

He was contemplating a response when Mike stepped onto the porch. He was wearing khakis, a dress shirt and a big goofy grin.

"Where are you going?" Ross asked.

"I have a date."

"With?"

Mike's grin grew broader. "Corinne."

"Corinne *Hawkins*?" Jack asked for clarity's sake.

"Yes. She's the only Corinne I know."

Jack shook his head. "No way. You can't date her. Not now."

"Why not? I like her. She likes me. There's a movie we both want to see and we're going to see it."

"But you're competing against her in the Battle of the Sexes."

"So what?"

"So you shouldn't be cavorting with the enemy."

"'Cavorting with the enemy'? You're losing your mind. It's just a good-natured exhibition designed to attract people to the rodeo. It's the Battle of the Sexes, not a battle to the death."

"I never said it was."

"The points won't count in the standings. It's just good fun."

"Maybe. But there's no way we can let them win."

"Did you hear what I said? It's just fun. I don't understand why you're taking it so seriously all of a sudden. No one else is."

"Audrey is."

Mike shrugged. "Then you're two of a kind. Corinne and I are only in it to have fun. And speaking of fun, I'm off. See you two later."

Mike jogged down the stairs and was in his car and down the street in a minute.

Jack shook his head. "It's a good thing he's going to medical school. He's not nearly as committed as he should be."

"Rodeo is only a *part* of life, Jack. It's not life," Ross said quietly. "And it certainly isn't worthy of losing someone you care for."

"So that means you aren't taking it seriously either? If only Geoff was here, he'd understand."

"Think so?" Ross shook his head.

"Does that mean I should expect you to start dating Brynn or Remi?"

"They're both beautiful, but no."

"Well, that's something," Jack said begrudgingly.

"What's really something is the way you didn't

include Audrey. I suppose as far as you're concerned, she's still off-limits."

Jack sputtered. Before he could reply, Ross was on his feet and walking away. When he reached the front door, he turned back and looked at him. "I get that you want to be Cowboy of the Year and break all of Geoff's records. And I truly hope you succeed. But don't lose sight of what's important. And definitely don't do it at a cost of something that could matter even more."

Needing fresh air, Jack sat on the porch swing and pondered Ross's words. He respected his brother and appreciated his point of view, but he was off by a mile. Jack wasn't looking for love or commitment. Sure, Audrey was great. And in another time and place, he would pursue her. But this was here and now. Time on the circuit was short and he only had a small window to make his mark before he was too old.

He'd always believed there was plenty of time to find love, but thinking about living his life without Audrey didn't hold much appeal. But she was a professional and she understood the sacrifices that were necessary to be the best. And he would settle for nothing less than being the best.

"Did you see what he posted?" Remi asked Audrey as they brushed their horses after training for the rodeo.

Audrey didn't need to ask her sister what *he* she was talking about. She already knew. For the past three days, Audrey and Jack had been engaged in a fierce social media battle. Their sparring had garnered plenty of interest and they and the Battle of the Sexes had been featured in a segment on the local news last night. Tickets for the Bronco Summer Family Rodeo were selling like hotcakes. They were definitely drawing attention to the event, although not the kind of attention Audrey had been looking for.

"No, and I don't want to see it," Audrey said. She was sick of Jack's posts and sicker still of the comments that he left on her posts. Although she did have to give him points for being clever. His sense of humor was definitely coming through, although she wouldn't admit that to anyone. She only begrudgingly admitted it to herself.

"I don't understand what went wrong between the two of you."

"How many times do I have to tell you there was nothing going on? There was no *two of us*. We went out a couple of times and had a few laughs. That doesn't constitute a relationship. Even a hopeless romantic like you has to see that."

"I'm not a hopeless romantic. I just have the ability to tell when two people are meant to be together. And I can see—"

Audrey rolled her eyes. "You don't have any special ability."

"—*and I can see* that you and Jack have something special. You belong together. Now, I'm not saying that you should get married—"

"Thank heaven for small favors."

"—but I think you should give a relationship a try. Maybe talk to him the next time you see him."

"Oh, I have a few words I'd like to say to him, but I don't think they're the words that you have in mind."

"You are so stubborn."

"Why? Because I won't cooperate with this fairy tale you've created for me? Because I won't chase after him? I don't know how many times or how many ways I have to tell you this. I'm not interested in Jack Burris. Period."

Remi nodded. "If you say so."

Audrey could feel the disappointment rolling off her sister, but such was life. She was pretty disappointed by the turn of events herself. "I do. And if you don't mind, I would prefer not to talk about Jack again."

"Fine."

"You guys finished?" Brynn asked as she and Corinne joined them. They'd been across the stables, caring for their own horses.

"Yes," Remi said.

She and Audrey stepped into the center aisle

and closed the stall doors behind them. The stable that had been recommended to house their horses was well run and had a good staff of grooms. Still, the sisters had been raised to care for their own horses, and that had helped them bond with the animals.

"You want to get some lunch?" Audrey asked.

"Sorry," Corinne said. "I'm meeting Mike."

"You two are awfully close," Remi said, smiling broadly at their baby sister. Clearly, Remi was happiest when someone was in a relationship. It didn't matter which sister it was. Oddly enough, she never seemed to fall in love herself. If she ever had, she'd managed to keep it a secret from the rest of them.

"We're just having fun."

"Really?" Remi asked.

Corinne grinned wickedly. "Lots of fun."

Remi laughed and Audrey and Brynn shook their heads.

"Seriously, though, we're taking things slowly. After all, we're both on the circuit and don't know when we'll meet up again. We're just enjoying the time we have together."

Although Corinne was looking at Remi, Audrey had a feeling that she was talking directly to her. But their situations were different. From everything Audrey could see, Mike respected Corinne's job. He didn't think he was automati-

KATHY DOUGLASS

cally a better rodeo rider simply because he was a man. Too bad Jack wasn't more like his brother.

They walked out together and got into their car. Audrey's sisters talked on the drive, but for the most part she was in her own little world.

Shortly after they got home, Mike arrived to pick up Corinne. Neither Brynn nor Remi was interested in going anywhere, so Audrey was on her own. After prowling the house for a few minutes, she grabbed her car keys and headed downtown.

She parked and then strolled down the street, stepping into the occasional boutique to look around.

As she wandered along the sidewalk, a new bracelet that she'd just purchased from Beaumont and Rossi's Fine Jewels dangling from her wrist, she wondered what it would have been like to grow up here. There was such a sense of community that seemed to envelop her. Oh, she knew no place was perfect, and even she had heard whispers about the divide between the haves of Bronco Heights and the have-nots of Bronco Valley. But even with that squabbling, this town still looked like a great place to live.

Although Audrey had grown up traveling the rodeo circuit and had for the most part enjoyed it, she and her sisters had been discussing the possibility of setting down roots in Bronco. But if they did, she would be living in the same town where Jack Burris had grown up. No doubt she would run into him occasionally.

The thought brought her up short and she stopped midstride. A person emerging from a shop hadn't expected her to stop and he bumped right into her.

She was about to apologize when she glanced up into Jack's face. The words stuck in her throat, and she could only stare at him. So many emotions shot through her that she couldn't hold on to one for more than an instant.

First, there was the shock and confusion that had her blinking, although she shouldn't have been surprised to see him. This was his hometown, after all. Then there was happiness that had her insides smiling, something she managed to keep her face from doing. This was quickly followed by fury for his sexist attitude. Worst was the stubborn desire to get closer to him.

"Oh. It's you," she said. She winced as she realized how the inane words must have sounded.

"In the flesh."

"What are you doing here?" Another ridiculous comment. One more for the hat trick.

"Why wouldn't I be here? I live here."

"What's that supposed to mean?"

His forehead wrinkled as if he was perplexed by her response. "It means just what it sounds like. I was born and raised in Bronco. I plan on buying a home of my own here when I retire from rodeo."

"And that's it. You're trying to tell me that you weren't inferring something else. Something to do with me."

"You know, Audrey, you are the most confusing woman I've ever met. You can take a simple statement and turn it inside out and upside down to suit your purposes. I have no idea what that purpose might be right now, so let me make it plain so that you can understand it. I was talking about me. Referring only to myself. You were the farthest thing from my mind when I spoke. Does that make it clear to you?"

"Perfectly." Way to make her feel like he wasn't the least bit interested in her. That wouldn't bother her so much if she was able to say the same about him. But she couldn't. He was on her mind more often than not.

When she did manage to force herself to think of something else, it took more effort than it should. And it was only a temporary victory. Her mind betrayed her when she slept, and she couldn't even dream without him showing up. It hurt knowing she didn't even cross his mind. And that pain made her angry. And reckless.

"But if I'm so far from your mind, why do you keep mentioning me on social media? If you're not tweeting about me, you're posting about me on Instagram or making some stupid TikTok video about me. I'm starting to think you're obsessed with me."

"What?" He sputtered and then his eyes narrowed. For a moment, it looked like the top of his head was going to blow off.

The smart thing to do would be to step away from him, but she wasn't feeling particularly smart at the moment. She was becoming more careless with every breath she took. Leaning closer, she poked him in his chest. It was just as hard as she remembered. "You heard me. You're turning into a regular cyber stalker. I've been wondering if I need to hire a bodyguard to protect me."

"What?" This time his voice filled with disbelief. And it was so loud, it came close to breaking the sound barrier.

"Excuse me," a woman said as she tried to pass them, and Audrey realized they were blocking the entrance to Bronco Java and Juice.

"Sorry," Audrey muttered and stepped aside. Now would be a good time to end the conversation and go on about her business. That's what a smart woman would do. Instead, she grabbed Jack's arm and pulled him down the street and into an alley where they would be out of the way of other pedestrians. She was furious with him, but at the same time, she couldn't help the desire that touching him had aroused in her.

"So are you going to say what's on your mind or not?" Jack said.

"Me?"

"You're the one who dragged me back here. So what do you want?" He smirked slyly. "Don't tell me you brought me back here to have your wicked way with me."

She sputtered. "Have my way with you? You should be so lucky. You're the one with the obsession, not me."

"Really? Shall we take a look at your social media? Every time I turn around, you're talking about me. Or commenting on my posts. If anyone is obsessed, it's you. I'm starting to think that you have a thing for me. If I come to your house, will I find my posters taped to your wall and covered with lipstick from where you kiss them?"

"What?" She was outraged at how close he came to the truth. She couldn't stop looking at the picture of them together, although she hadn't gone so far as to kiss his image. "You must have the strongest horse in the world."

"What does that even mean?"

"It means your head and ego are so outsized, a regular horse couldn't possibly carry it around and still perform."

"You got a lot of nerve, lady, talking about somebody's ego. You… You…"

He had clearly used up all of his brain power because he seemed to be stuck on that one word and repeated it several more times.

They glared at each other, their chests rising and falling, neither of them speaking. And then they were kissing. She had no idea how it had happened or who had made the first move. One minute, they were arguing. The next, they were in each other's arms, kissing for all they were worth. The emotions that she'd kept bottled up inside her burst forth, taking complete control. She felt his tongue swipe across her lips and she opened her mouth to him. In an instant, their tongues were tangoing. She loved the taste of him, and a moan of pleasure escaped her lips.

She was practically crawling inside his skin, but she couldn't get close enough to him. She flung her arms around his neck, and he wrapped his arms more tightly around her waist, pressing her against his body. His muscles were wonderfully hard against her, and her stomach did a topsy-turvy flip at the contact. The heat from his body encircled her, setting her aflame. His hands were gentle as they caressed her back, urging her to give her pent-up desire free rein. Everything inside her screamed to get closer to him. She wanted more of his kiss. She wanted more of *him*. Time seemed to stand still as she gave herself over to his kiss, dangerously close to losing all control.

In the distance, a car horn blew, the sound bringing her back to reality. She was in downtown Bronco making out with Jack Burris. Standing in the middle of Main Street where anyone could see them. True, they'd stepped off of the main drag, but they weren't exactly hidden.

Audrey snatched away, resisting the part of her that would be perfectly happy necking with Jack no matter who saw, and wiped a hand across her mouth. "What was that?"

"It was a kiss. Or is that something so foreign to you that you didn't know that? Surely, you've been kissed at least once in your life, Audrey. But then, given your caustic personality, maybe I shouldn't assume that."

"You. You. Jerk."

He laughed. "You accost me and I'm the jerk."

"I didn't accost you."

"No? You dragged me into this alley and pounced on me. If that's not accosting me, I don't know what is."

"I couldn't drag you if I tried. I asked you to come and you came willingly."

"So you could jump on me."

"I. Brought. You. Here. So. We. Could. *Talk.*"

"So talk. What is it that you're so desperate to tell me?"

Her mind went blank. She couldn't think, not when she was still reeling from the kiss and his taste lingered in her mouth. Her knees were still wobbly and it took supreme effort to not melt into a puddle at his feet. Despite how annoyed she was with him, she would kiss him again if he made a move in her direction. And that bit of knowledge made her even angrier with him. And herself. She hated the weakness her desire for him created. Especially since he appeared to be completely unbothered by the kiss.

"Nothing, Jack. I have nothing to say to you." She pulled herself to her full height, painfully aware that even in heels, she wasn't able to meet him eye-to-eye. But then, she really didn't want to see whatever was in his eyes. And she really didn't want him to see the residue of her yearning that no doubt remained in hers.

She brushed past him, doing her best not to touch him. Even so, she felt a tingling down her spine as she stepped around him, determined not to let him know just how much his nearness affected her as she strode down the street and to her car.

Jack put his hands on his hips and then leaned back, staring at the sky. What in the world had he just done? *He'd kissed Audrey Hawkins.* Why?

Okay, not why. He knew why he'd kissed her. He was attracted to her and had wanted to kiss her for a long time. Perhaps from the very first moment he'd laid eyes on her. Maybe sooner. Maybe it was the first time he'd heard her laugh. It truly didn't matter when he'd first wanted to kiss her. The fact was he'd finally done it.

And it was the worst thing he could have done.

Oh, not from a physical standpoint. Kissing her had been heaven on earth. Holding her in his arms as their lips met and their tongues tangled had far exceeded any experience he'd shared with a woman. And if the moment had occurred in another way, he would be thrilled. Under other circumstances, he'd be in search of the nearest bed so he could make love to her. But after the way he'd just behaved, getting close to her again wasn't in his immediate future. Maybe not in the distant future either.

Why had he taunted her? And why had he acted as if he hadn't loved kissing her? Hadn't dreamed of that very thing every night since he'd met her? Would he do it again if given half a chance? Hell yes. Well, there was no going back and fixing things between them now. Perhaps it was for the best. Audrey was a distraction. More than that, she was now the competition. Those were reasons enough to keep his distance from her.

But that was easier said than done. She was always on his mind, haunting him no matter what he was doing. If he'd hoped by kissing her he'd get her out of his system, he'd be disappointed. Despite how things ended and the harsh words they'd exchanged, he still wanted her.

One thing was certain. He couldn't leave things as they were. He'd hurt her and she deserved an apology. But with the desire still surging inside him, he didn't trust himself to be around her at the moment. He'd only kiss her again. They'd both be at the rodeo tomorrow. He'd set things straight then. Hopefully by then he wouldn't be consumed with lust.

His mother was in the kitchen cooking dinner when he got home. He poured a glass of lemonade and then leaned against the counter. "Need help?"

"You could set the table for three."

"Mike and Ross not around?"

"Mike has a date and Ross is meeting a few friends. So it'll just be us and Dad. And maybe you can tell us why you look like you've lost your best friend."

"I'm fine."

"Are you sure? Because I haven't seen you look like this since you and Abby broke up."

"Mom, I was a sophomore in high school. That was thirteen years ago."

"I know. But you loved that girl with your

entire fifteen-year-old heart. If you're having woman trouble, I'm here if you want to talk. I give great advice. If you don't believe me, ask Geoff."

Jack's brother had been close to blowing it with Stephanie. If not for their mother's wise counsel, he would no doubt still be trying to figure out what he'd done wrong and how to get Stephanie back into his life. But given the fact that Geoff had ended up engaged, a fate Jack wanted to avoid, it would be in his best interest to avoid his mother's advice. He only wanted forgiveness, not a fiancée.

"I'll keep that in mind. But if it's okay with you and Dad, I think I'll skip dinner tonight. I'm not all that hungry."

"Suit yourself. But remember loss of appetite is one of the first signs of being in love. Or a broken heart."

"Got it." But being in love wasn't what ailed him. At least he hoped not.

Chapter Nine

What was going on? Audrey felt eyes on her as she and her sisters made their way to the dressing room of the convention center on the opening day of the rodeo. Unlike the day of the photo shoot when they'd changed behind screens in the arena, there was actually a real dressing room set up for the women to change. One of the other women in there giggled and stared at her.

"What are you looking at?" Audrey's voice came out sharper than she'd intended. Thanks to the argument with Jack and the hot kiss that she'd relived over and over, she hadn't gotten much sleep last night, and she was irritable. She didn't have the patience to deal with whatever foolishness was going on.

The other woman—Linda? No, it was Lydia—gave Audrey a strange look as if trying to decide how to respond. Audrey had a reputation as a fierce competitor, but she was known to be a kind person. She blew out a breath. "Sorry. I didn't mean to bite your head off."

"Okay. I guess you haven't seen it."

"What *it*?"

"The picture of you and Jack Burris."

"We took a lot of pictures to advertise the rodeo. They've been rolling them out a few at a time."

"I don't think this is one of them. Unless making out in public was part of the plan."

"What?"

Lydia handed over her phone. Audrey looked at the screen and gasped at the image there. She and Jack were locked in a passionate embrace, kissing. Their naked need practically jumped off the screen. Who had taken that picture? And how? Had a passerby taken it? Had they been captured by a street camera? No. Neither of those things made sense. They'd been too far out of the way for someone to just stumble along and see them.

One thought came to her mind. She tried to push it back, but it wouldn't be banished. Reluctantly, she accepted it. She'd been set up. There was no other explanation. What were the odds that Jack would just happen to be on the same street as she'd been at the very same time? Slim to none. And then he'd goaded and taunted her. Then, when she'd been revved up, he'd kissed her, all the while knowing that they were being photographed.

Was this his way of trying to get inside her head in a desperate attempt to gain an advantage over her? Well, it wasn't going to work. He could play whatever mind games he wanted, but she wouldn't be knocked off her center. She was a professional. She gave Lydia back the phone and then went to change.

"Wow. You and Jack," Remi said, looking at her phone. "There's a lot of comments on the post."

Despite telling herself not to, Audrey couldn't help but ask, "What are they saying?"

"That they could tell that there was a romance brewing between the two of you just by looking at the posters. Apparently everyone is rooting for the two of you to get together."

"Well, they're going to be disappointed. After this stunt, there's no way that Jack and I will ever be together. I'll never forgive him for being so underhanded."

"Are you saying that Jack was behind this?"

"How else do you explain it?"

"I don't know, but I don't think you're being fair. And if you don't mind my saying so, in that picture you look like you're enjoying yourself."

She had been. That kiss had been beyond pleasurable. But that was beside the point. A relationship between her and Jack could never work. He was a cowboy and their lifestyles didn't lend themselves to successful romances.

She looked at her watch. There were a few minutes before start time. If she hurried, she could catch Jack and let him know just what she thought of the dirty little trick he'd played on her.

Although her sisters tried to convince her that Jack might have been as unsuspecting as she'd been, she just couldn't believe that he'd been caught off guard. She didn't know why she needed to cast him as the villain in this little play, but she did. Then it hit her. As long as he was the one at fault, she didn't have to consider her growing feelings for him. If he was the bad guy, that made him off-limits. And she needed for him to be off-limits.

The men's changing area was located across the hall and down the corridor, and as she walked, she picked up her pace, fueled by her anger. She was practically running by the time she reached the door. It was closed, so she pounded on it.

A cowboy opened the door, took one look at

her and smiled. Had he seen the picture? "How can I help you?"

"Is Jack Burris inside?"

"I'll get him for you." He turned and then yelled Jack's name. Looking back at her, he continued, "He's on his way."

"Thank you."

While she waited, she rehearsed what she was going to say. She would read him the riot act and let him know how disappointed she was with his sneaky tactics. But when the door opened and he stood there looking like God had intended cowboys to look, every word of her tirade fled from her mind and all she could do was gawk at him.

Although she'd seen him dressed in his gear at the photo shoot, there was something different about knowing that he was about to compete that raised his sex appeal to another level. Realizing that her thoughts had betrayed her once again made her angrier. She shoved her phone in his face and waited while he looked at the screen.

"I've already seen that picture."

"How could you?"

"How could I not? Everybody and their brother has shown it to me."

"That's not what I mean. How could you set me up like this?"

"You think I arranged that?" He shook his head. "No way. And if you thought about it before coming down here to confront me, you'd know there's no way I could have."

"I've done nothing but think about it since I saw the picture. And somehow the idea that you aren't the one behind it hasn't occurred to me yet."

He gripped her shoulders and gave them a gentle shake. "Think about it. You're the one who pulled me into the alley. Maybe you're the one who had the photographer waiting and set me up."

"Don't be ridiculous. I didn't even know I was going to run into you."

"And yet somehow you think that I knew I was going to run into you? How does that even make sense?"

He had a point. And it did sound ridiculous when he put it like that. It was just that it was so hard to think rationally when he was involved. Thinking about Jack scrambled her brains. "Who do you think took the picture?"

"I have no idea," he said wearily. "It could have been a random passerby. Everybody has a camera on their phones. Or maybe some paparazzo is following us around. Who knows? But I swear to you, it wasn't me. I wouldn't set you up like that."

His voice rang with sincerity. Even so, she stared at him, trying to see the truth in his eyes. They were troubled, but there was no deception there. She realized that Jack would never do something underhanded like this. She was ashamed for thinking it, even for a moment. "I believe you. I'm sorry for accusing you. It's just that this is embarrassing for me."

"I'm not exactly pleased, but I'm not embarrassed. I won't try to tell you how to feel. And I am sorry for not being able to control myself. If I hadn't kissed you like that, there wouldn't be a picture of us together."

She could have let him wallow in his guilt, but that wasn't fair. "You didn't make me kiss you. I was just as into it as you were. But I feel like someone is playing me and I don't like it."

"I understand. I'm not a big fan of the intrusion either."

They stood there in awkward silence for a moment. Jack looked at his watch and then blew out a breath. "Listen. The rodeo is about to start, so we both need to finish getting ready."

Of course. Because that was the *professional* thing to do. She turned to go. "See you later."

Jack watched as Audrey walked away from him, trying his best to control his feelings. Despite the fact that they'd just had a civilized conversation, there was still a lot of tension between them. Who would have believed that a few short days ago they'd actually had fun together? Looking at the state of affairs between them now, it could have been two other people who'd shared meals and gone driving in his car.

Get your act together. He grabbed his hat and went to check on his horse, making sure that everything was perfect for his ride. He pulled on the reins and stirrups. When he was assured that everything was in order, he rejoined the other cowboys to await his turn to ride.

He generally liked to spend the time before he competed alone so he could envision his ride. His brothers, as usual, gave him his space. Now, though, instead of picturing how he would move on Spirit in the roping event, he kept seeing Audrey's face. She'd been furious when she'd come over to him. More than that, she'd been hurt and embarrassed about the picture. He was none too pleased about it, either, but you didn't see him making wild accusations. He couldn't believe she'd actually thought he could pull a stunt like that. Despite the fact that he'd convinced her of his innocence, it still stung to know that she'd even entertained the idea for a minute. Clearly, she didn't know him as well as he'd thought she did.

Not liking the direction of his thoughts, he sought out Mike and Ross, who were lounging in a corner of the dressing room. As usual, they were relaxed and shooting the breeze while they awaited their turns to compete.

Although Ross and Mike were professional and always tried their best, they weren't as serious about rodeo as Jack and Geoff were. Mike had been clear that although he enjoyed rodeo, it was only a means to an end. He was participating to earn money for medical school. He had managed to graduate from college with double degrees in biology and human physiology while traveling on the circuit.

Ross had been a bit more devoted than Mike, but even he was starting to talk about quitting and opening a business, using his winnings as seed money. Jack didn't quite understand their choices, but he respected them. And he was determined to reach the pinnacle of rodeo. Soon.

"What's up?" Ross asked, scooting over on the bench so Jack could sit down.

"It's that picture."

"What about it?"

"Audrey actually accused me of being behind it."

"Oh," Ross said and then glanced over at Mike.

"What? You don't sound nearly as outraged as you should be."

"Perhaps because of all the posts you've made on social media. It's clear that you were trying to get inside her head."

"I wouldn't stoop to doing something like this."

"I know that. It was probably a fan. Or one of

the organizers. They have really been playing up the whole romance between the two of you for publicity."

"There is no romance between us."

Mike, who had been silent up until this point, guffawed. "No? Then what the heck was that kiss about? Because the fire is clearly there. I'm surprised my phone didn't melt from the heat between the two of you."

"Knock it off," Jack said. He should have known better than to come over here.

"He's not wrong," Ross said. "It's obvious that the two of you are attracted to each other. I really don't see the problem."

"You wouldn't," Jack grumbled.

"And I'm up," Mike said.

"Good luck," Jack and Ross said in unison.

They followed Mike to the edge of the ring so they could watch him ride. Even when they competed in the same events, they always watched, looking for ways to help each other improve. And, of course, to cheer one another on.

Mike was absolutely fantastic. He received the highest score of his career and was beaming when he returned.

"Way to go," Ross said. "You're at the top of the leaderboard."

"Good job," Jack said. "That's the best you've ever done."

Mike nodded. "I attribute it all to my relationship with Corinne."

Jack had a feeling he was directing that comment to him, but he ignored it. Their situations weren't remotely the same. Corinne and Mike were two happy-go-lucky people. Jack and Audrey were fierce competitors. He hoped she did well in her events against the other women, but when they went head-to-head in two days, he planned on coming out on top. Second place would never be good enough.

Ross took his turn and did well, although he didn't get a personal best, as Mike had done. "Perhaps I should date one of the other Hawkins sisters so I can get a career-high score, too," he said as he rejoined his brothers.

"There are still two free sisters," Mike joked.

"According to Jack, there are *three* sisters to choose from," Ross said. "I mean since he isn't involved with Audrey."

Jack glared and stalked away without responding. He didn't want to think about Audrey. More than that, he didn't want to think about Ross with Audrey. Ross had always been the charming brother, the one who women flocked around. Ross had a different woman in every town. Jack was sure that if Ross wanted to, he could have Audrey on his arm in no time flat.

Jack shoved the thought out of his mind. He

had a competition to win. He wouldn't be able to do that with Audrey consuming all of his thoughts. That was why he had wanted to end things with her in the first place.

He stood in line and then got on the bronco he'd drawn to ride. When he was set, Jack nodded and the pen gate swung open. The horse bucked and Jack had to make adjustments on the fly to stay on for the required eight seconds. At the end of his ride, he jumped off the back of the bronc and the cheers of the crowd followed him backstage. When he got there, he shook his head and tossed his hat to the ground in frustration.

"Not your best ride," Mike said. The Burris brothers were just as honest with each other as they were supportive.

"Not even close."

"It's just the preliminary round," Ross pointed out. "You needed to stay on and make it to the final round, which you did. And with your score, you can still come out on top."

"True." Jack knew that he hadn't been mathematically eliminated. But he also knew that he was going to have to be at the top of his game to have a realistic chance of winning.

"Of course, you might want to get yourself a good luck charm like I have," Mike said, winking.

"I don't need luck," Jack said.

"Maybe not. And on that note, I'm going to

find a seat so I can watch Corinne and her sisters compete. You coming?"

Jack and Ross nodded and followed Mike into the auditorium, sitting in seats that had been reserved for competitors. It was rare for Jack to watch the other riders, but he wanted to know what he was up against in his competition with Audrey. He also wanted to be able to support her and cheer her on, even if she wouldn't know he was there.

They watched as the women competed at calf roping. Jack had to admit that the women displayed well-honed skill. He noticed that when Corinne rode, Mike sat stock-still with his fingers crossed. If he breathed, Jack wasn't aware of it. When she was done, Mike cheered and jumped to his feet. He put his fingers in his mouth and let out a loud whistle. There was no mistaking who he wanted to win.

Remi and Brynn each rode, and the brothers applauded their efforts. And then it was Audrey's turn. She was the last rider, and as the event had progressed, Jack found himself growing nervous on her behalf. That was ridiculous. Naturally, he wanted her to do well, but the stress he felt was outsized and uncalled for. He inhaled deeply and tried to calm his rattled nerves.

When her ride was over, Jack breathed a sigh of relief and all of the tension eased from his

FREE BOOKS GIVEAWAY

2 FREE ROMANCE BOOKS!

2 FREE WHOLESOME ROMANCE BOOKS!

GET UP TO FOUR FREE BOOKS & TWO FREE GIFTS WORTH OVER $20!

We pay for everything!

See Details Inside

YOU pick your books – WE pay for everything.

You get up to FOUR New Books and TWO Mystery Gifts...absolutely FREE

Dear Reader,

I am writing to announce the launch of a huge **FREE BOOKS GIVEAWAY**... and to let you know that YOU are entitled to choose up to FOUR fantastic books that WE pay for.

Try **Harlequin® Special Edition** books featuring comfort and strength in the support of loved ones and enjoying the journey no mader what life throws your way.

Try **Harlequin® Heartwarming™ Larger-Print** books featuring uplifting stories where the bonds of friendship, family and community unite.

Or TRY BOTH!

In return, we ask just one favor: Would you please participate in our brief Reader Survey? We'd love to hear from you.

This FREE BOOKS GIVEAWAY means that your introductory shipment is completely free, <u>even the shipping</u>! If you decide to continue, you can look forward to curated monthly shipments of brand-new books from your selected series, always at a discount off the cover price! <u>Plus you can cancel any time</u>. Who could pass up a deal like that?

Sincerely

Pam Powers

Pam Powers
For Harlequin Reader Service

Complete the survey below and return it today to receive up to 4 FREE BOOKS and FREE GIFTS guaranteed!

▼ DETACH AND MAIL CARD TODAY! ▼

FREE BOOKS GIVEAWAY
Reader Survey

1

Do you prefer stories with happy endings?

◯ YES   ◯ NO

2

Do you share your favorite books with friends?

◯ YES   ◯ NO

3

Do you often choose to read instead of watching TV?

◯ YES   ◯ NO

YES! Please send me my Free Rewards, consisting of **2 Free Books from each series I select** and **Free Mystery Gifts**. I understand that I am under no obligation to buy anything, no purchase necessary see terms and conditions for details.

❏ Harlequin® Special Edition (235/335 HDL GRQ6)
❏ Harlequin® Heartwarming™ Larger-Print (161/361 HDL GRQ6)
❏ Try Both (235/335 & 161/361 HDL GRRJ)

FIRST NAME   LAST NAME

ADDRESS

APT.#   CITY

STATE/PROV.   ZIP/POSTAL CODE

EMAIL ❏ Please check this box if you would like to receive newsletters and promotional emails from Harlequin Enterprises ULC and its affiliates. You can unsubscribe anytime.

Your Privacy – Your information is being collected by Harlequin Enterprises ULC, operating as Harlequin Reader Service. For a complete summary of the information we collect, how we use this information and to whom it is disclosed, please visit our privacy notice located at https://corporate.harlequin.com/privacy-notice. From time to time we may also exchange your personal information with reputable third parties. If you wish to opt out of this sharing of your personal information, please visit www.readerservice.com/consumerschoice or call 1-800-873-8635. **Notice to California Residents** – Under California law, you have specific rights to control and access your data. For more information on these rights and how to exercise them, visit https://corporate.harlequin.com/california-privacy.

© 2022 HARLEQUIN ENTERPRISES ULC
® and ™ are trademarks owned and used by the trademark owner and/or its licensee. Printed in the U.S.A.

SE/HW-122-FBG22

HARLEQUIN Reader Service —**Terms and Conditions:**

Accepting your 2 free books and 2 free gifts (gifts valued at approximately $10.00 retail) places you under no obligation to buy anything. You may keep the books and gifts and return the shipping statement marked "cancel." If you do not cancel, approximately one month later we'll send you more books from the series you have chosen, and bill you at our low, subscribers-only discount price. Harlequin® Special Edition books consist of 6 books per month and cost $5.24 each in the U.S. or $5.99 each in Canada, a savings of at least 13% off the cover price. Harlequin® Heartwarming™ Larger-Print books consist of 4 books per month and cost just $5.99 each in the U.S. or $6.49 each in Canada, a savings of at least 20% off the cover price. It's quite a bargain! Shipping and handling is just 50¢ per book in the U.S. and $1.25 per book in Canada.* You may return any shipment at our expense and cancel at any time by calling the number below — or you may continue to receive monthly shipments at our low, subscribers-only discount price plus shipping and handling. *Terms and prices subject to change without notice. Prices do not include sales taxes which will be charged (if applicable) based on your state or country of residence. Canadian residents will be charged applicable taxes. Offer not valid in Quebec. Books received may not be as shown. All orders subject to approval. Credit or debit balances in a customer's account(s) may be offset by any other outstanding balance owed by or to the customer. Please allow 3 to 4 weeks for delivery. Offer available while quantities last. **Your Privacy** – Your information is being collected by Harlequin Enterprises ULC, operating as Harlequin Reader Service. For a complete summary of the information we collect, how we use this information and to whom it is disclosed, please visit our privacy notice located at https://corporate.harlequin.com/privacy-notice. From time to time we may also exchange your personal information with reputable third parties. If you wish to opt out of this sharing of your personal information, please visit https://www.readerservice.com/consumerschoice or call 1-800-873-8635. **Notice to California Residents** – Under California law, you have specific rights to control and access your data. For more information on these rights and how to exercise them, visit https://corporate.harlequin.com/california-privacy.

▲ If offer card is missing write to: Harlequin Reader Service, P.O. Box 1341, Buffalo, NY 14240-8531 or visit www.ReaderService.com ▲

BUSINESS REPLY MAIL

FIRST-CLASS MAIL PERMIT NO. 717 BUFFALO, NY

POSTAGE WILL BE PAID BY ADDRESSEE

HARLEQUIN READER SERVICE
PO BOX 1341
BUFFALO NY 14240-8571

NO POSTAGE
NECESSARY
IF MAILED
IN THE
UNITED STATES

body. Even from his seat in the audience, he was able to see her face. She was smiling, but it didn't reach her eyes. He could see the disappointment in her face. She hadn't performed her best, either, and her score was in the middle of the pack.

The brothers remained in their seats as the stadium emptied. A few fans recognized them, and they posed for pictures and signed autographs. Once they were done, they returned backstage. Mike headed for the women's area to meet up with Corinne, and Jack and Ross trailed behind him for a reason that Jack didn't quite understand.

The Hawkins sisters were on their way out of their dressing room and they met in the hallway. While Jack's brothers and Audrey's sisters greeted each other warmly, Audrey and Jack merely nodded at one another and kept their distance.

"What are you ladies doing for the rest of the day?" Mike asked. Although his question was a general one, he was looking at Corinne. *Yep, he had it bad.*

She looked at her sisters, who shrugged, and then back at Mike. "Nothing."

"Do you want to go by Doug's and get something to eat? Our treat."

"Sure."

Jack was tempted to poke Mike in his side really hard. How could he just volunteer them to take the sisters out for a late lunch without consulting him first? Not that he minded paying for it. He just wasn't ready to hang out with Audrey. Things were way too tense between them. And since the very thought of her made it difficult for him to focus on anything other than her, spending more time with her obviously wasn't good for his mental health or for his performance. But he couldn't back out without looking like a jerk or a lovesick fool, so he swallowed his objection and joined the group.

When they arrived at Doug's, Jack parked and went inside. He'd driven alone, and though he was loathe to admit it, he'd missed Audrey's company.

They shoved a couple of tables together and sat down. He didn't know how the others managed it, but somehow, he and Audrey ended up side by side again. He pulled out her chair and held it for her.

"Thank you," she said, sitting.

The scent of her shampoo teased him, reminding him of the fiery kiss they'd shared and rekindling his desire. He shoved it away. Hadn't his body gotten him in enough trouble already? "Control yourself."

"Talking to yourself again?" Audrey asked, smirking.

"How do you know I wasn't talking to you?"

She grinned and his heart thudded so hard it

might have been attempting to escape his chest. She crossed her heart, drawing his eyes to her gorgeous breasts. "I promise to be on my best behavior. I swear to eat only my food, that is unless yours looks better than mine, then all bets are off."

He laughed. "No worries there."

Although Doug had a nice spread for the Sunday brunch, his food the rest of the week was typical bar fare. They dined on chicken wings, fries, mozzarella sticks and fried mushrooms, chasing it down with pitchers of sodas.

After an uneasy beginning and a few false starts, Audrey and Jack joined in the laughter and conversation. Despite all appearances of getting along, he was painfully aware that although she was quite friendly with his brothers, apart from their initial interaction, Audrey didn't engage directly in conversation with him.

That bothered him more than it should have. After all, he was the one who'd suggested that they keep their distance. Even so, her attitude kept him awake all night.

Chapter Ten

"Hey, what's with the commotion?" Ross asked as he got out of his car at the convention center the next morning.

Jack grabbed his hat from the passenger seat of his car and then looked in the direction his brother was pointing. There were dozens of people milling around, staring at flyers that had been posted all over the outside of the building. He hoped that it didn't have anything to do with him and Audrey. The last thing he wanted was another confrontation. "I don't know, but I have a feeling we're about to find out."

Mike joined them and they approached a

group of people. Jack recognized one of his former high school classmates. "What are you staring at, Bill?"

"Take a look for yourself." Bill handed over a flyer with three words written in bold letters.

Remember Bobby Stone.

"'Remember Bobby Stone.' What's that supposed to mean?" Jack asked.

"Your guess is as good as mine," Bill said. "These flyers are plastered all over the place. But apart from these three words, there's no information."

"Weird," Jack said. He handed the flyer to his brothers, who looked at it and then handed it back.

"Good luck in there," their friend said. "I'll be cheering for you."

"Thanks."

"And of course, I'll be cheering for your new girlfriend," he said, giving Jack a nudge. "Audrey's quite the looker."

Jack didn't bother saying that Audrey wasn't his girl. He knew Bill wouldn't believe it. No doubt he'd seen the picture of the two of them kissing. In fact, if there was someone who had missed it, Jack had yet to meet them. There had been another segment about the "Rodeo Sweethearts," as everyone now referred to them, on one of those entertainment television shows last night. He and Audrey were now the unofficial king and queen of the rodeo. Someone had filmed the two of them while they'd been talking outside the men's dressing room yesterday, adding fuel to the fire. He hadn't seen anyone lurking about, so he didn't know who to blame. But then, he hadn't been looking for anyone either.

A gossip magazine had posted a picture from that encounter on its front page. The picture had made it appear that they were having an intensely emotional conversation, which they had been. But the caption had made it seem as if they'd shared a tender moment as opposed to the heated argument it had actually been. Well, there was one good thing. Audrey couldn't accuse him of setting her up that time since she'd sought him out. Of course, logic hadn't worked the first time, which was why she'd come to his dressing room in the first place.

He wondered if someone was following them. He wasn't a particularly private person, but he wasn't a fan of the paparazzi either. But since he didn't know who—if anyone—was behind the surveilling, he was powerless to put a stop to it. There was no proof that this was a coordinated effort. More than one person could be photographing them and selling the pictures. With every phone being a camera, it wouldn't be hard to do.

He shook his head. It didn't matter. He needed to focus on today's events. Thinking about the situation with Audrey would only lead to another poor performance.

"Let me have that," Katy, Chuck's assistant, said as she approached them.

"What? This flyer?"

"Yes." She took the paper and then balled it into a wad and shoved it into a bag slung over her shoulder. From the looks of it, she had a few dozen flyers in her bag. And there were still many more on the convention center walls as well as light posts in the area.

"What's this all about?" Mike asked.

"Somebody's idea of a sick joke," she said. "And they're all over the place. It must have taken hours to hang up these things. I have no idea how he managed it, but there are some taped on the walls inside, even in the washrooms. I've got a team trying to get rid of them before the crowds arrive."

"Good luck," Jack said before he and his brothers went inside, where they ran into the Hawkins sisters. Audrey held a flyer in her hand, so it was easy to guess what they'd been discussing. Since they weren't from here, they were probably more confused than the people who lived in Bronco.

"Hi," Mike said, greeting the sisters on behalf of the brothers.

"Have you seen this?" Audrey asked.

"Yes," Jack answered.

"What does it mean? Who is Bobby Stone and why should we remember him?"

"I don't think the flyer was intended for you since you aren't from Bronco."

"I kind of figured that out on my own. But still, who is Bobby Stone?"

"Bobby Stone was a guy who used to live in Bronco," Jack said. The doors to the convention center had been opened and people began to swarm around them as they made their way to the seats or the vendors, who were selling everything from T-shirts to hats to belt buckles.

"Let's get out of the way," Jack said, leading them to a secluded corner.

The Hawkins sisters looked at him eagerly and it took supreme effort not to stare at Audrey. She looked so sexy in her fitted jeans and blue T-shirt imprinted with a little girl wearing a crown.

"Don't leave us hanging," Remi said, dragging his attention back to the present. "Tell us about this Bobby Stone."

"Do you remember that chair behind the tape at Doug's?"

"Yes. We noticed it when we had brunch there," Brynn said.

"I thought it was weird, but since I've seen a lot of weird things on the road, I figured it was one more oddity and didn't give it a second thought," Audrey said, and her sisters nodded in agreement.

"Well, there are people who believe that chair is haunted and that anyone who sits there is doomed. At least, to hear Doug tell it. Ask him about it the next time you go in there."

"What's the chair got to do with Bobby Stone?"

"Well, Bobby sat there."

"And?"

Jack shook his head. "I think I'm telling the story all wrong. Let me start at the beginning."

He was usually a lot clearer than this. But then, on those occasions, Audrey wasn't looking at him with curious brown eyes and a smile curving her full lips. Even though she wasn't standing overly close to him, when he inhaled, he got a whiff of her scent and it was just enough to drive him wild. The fact that their siblings were around didn't do anything to cool his desire. He wanted to kiss her and hold her in his arms as he had the other day.

"So are you going to tell us?" Remi asked. Her eyes twinkled as if she could read his mind and knew that her sister's nearness was distracting him. Apparently, he was more transparent than he wanted to believe.

"Right. Bobby was a good guy. None of us knew him very well, but we saw him around town whenever we came back home. He might have drunk a little more than he should have, but other than that, he was a regular guy. Anyhow, a few years ago, he died in a freak accident. He'd been hiking on the trail. He had a heart attack and fell off a cliff. At least, that's what people think happened because his body was never found. There are some people, Doug included, who believe he met his demise because he sat on the haunted chair a couple of days before the accident."

"Wow," Audrey said.

"That's some tale," Corinne added.

"Do you believe the chair is haunted?" Audrey asked.

"No. I'm not the superstitious type."

"Besides, our big brother, Geoff, sat on the chair last Christmas when he was in town for the rodeo and nothing untoward happened to him," Mike added.

"Really? Didn't you say he injured his shoulder in an accident in this arena?" Brynn asked. "Wasn't that why you guys didn't want to pose on the bleachers?"

"That happened *before* he sat on the chair," Jack clarified. "Nothing bad happened after he sat on the chair."

"Unless you count getting engaged and no longer being a free man as something bad," Ross joked.

"We consider that lucky," Remi said.

"Speak for yourself," Audrey grumbled.

"But why would someone post the signs now? Does today's date have a special meaning?"

Corinne asked. "Or have flyers been posted before?"

"This is the first time that I'm aware of," Jack said. "And it's not an anniversary of any sort, so I have no idea why someone would do this now."

"Well, I hope his family isn't hurt by this reminder," Remi said. "That would be too cruel."

"True," Jack said. After a few moments of silence, he blew out a breath. This awkwardness between him and Audrey was getting to him. He'd tried to put her out of his mind, but that was easier said than done. Especially when she was always close enough to touch and yet completely out of his reach.

"We need to get going so we can get ready for our events. Good luck," Audrey said, her gaze encompassing him and his brothers.

"You, too."

He watched as Audrey and her sisters headed toward their dressing room, and then he turned and walked with his brothers to theirs. Despite himself, he smiled. Audrey had wished him good luck.

"What's going on with you and Jack?" Brynn said the moment they were inside the changing room. The four of them were the only ones inside at the moment so they could talk freely.

"Really? You're asking me that?" Audrey asked.

Brynn might be a mother hen, but she had already made her feelings about Jack clear. She wasn't the type to revisit a conversation once it was over and done, so this question was unexpected. "Why?"

"Because you're off your game. Of the four of us, you are the most dedicated and the most competitive. And, honestly, the most talented. But after yesterday's performance, it's clear that something is bothering you. It doesn't take a genius to know that Jack has gotten inside your head. Is it the whole Battle of the Sexes thing?"

"No."

"Then what is it? And don't waste my time or yours saying that it's nothing."

Audrey sighed and dropped onto a chair in front of the wall of mirrors. "I guess it is Jack. One minute he's Mr. Kind and Considerate, sweeping me off my feet. The next he's telling me that we can't see each other because it's not professional. As if I'm not professional. Then he turns around and kisses me like there's no tomorrow. He's so unpredictable. And you know I don't like not knowing what's going to happen."

"You mean you don't like not controlling what's going to happen."

"Potato, po-tah-to."

"I've never known you to let a man get to you this way. What's so different about Jack Burris?"

"I don't know. Despite all of his flaws, there's

something about him that just connects with me. I feel like he really gets me. It's wonderful and scary and aggravating all at once."

"Oh, no. Please don't tell me that you've fallen in love with him."

The very thought made Audrey's heart pound so hard she thought it might burst from her chest. There was no way she could be in love with Jack Burris. Was there? Of course not. She barely knew him. True, she'd felt so good when she was with him. There was something so comforting about him. At least, when he wasn't annoying her.

"Your lack of a response is making me nervous," Brynn said.

"I didn't answer because the idea is too ridiculous to deserve a response. No, I'm not in love with him."

"And if you were, would you admit it to me?" Brynn raised an eyebrow.

Audrey laughed at the expression on her sister's face. "Not in this lifetime."

"That's what I thought."

Another competitor walked into the dressing room, putting an end to the conversation. Not that there was anything left to be said. She had a job to do, and she needed to focus on that. Yesterday she hadn't performed up to her usual standard, but today would be different.

She dressed in her jeans, boots and deep purple

satin blouse with light purple fringe, brushed her hair into a slick ponytail, then put on her purple cowboy hat. Wearing one of her favorite outfits gave her an added level of confidence.

Today she was competing in the barrel racing, so after she was dressed she went to the pen to check on her horse, LemonDrop. Audrey loved her horse with her entire heart. They'd been a team for two years and they understood each other. LemonDrop only needed to be nudged a bit to take the turns like a pro. Since they'd been together, Audrey had come in first in nearly seventy-five percent of their events. In those events where she hadn't been first, she'd placed second or third, often losing by less than a second.

"Today is going to be our day," Audrey said. She pulled purple ribbon from her pocket and then braided her horse's tail, tying it with the ribbon. When she was done, she patted the horse. "You are going to be the prettiest girl out there."

"I don't know about that."

Audrey turned and spotted Jack, who was standing mere feet from her. How had he managed to sneak up on her? She was generally so aware of his presence whenever he was around. "Oh, no? I suppose you think your horse is prettier."

"Than yours? Well, yes, that goes without saying, but that's not who I was talking about."

"Then who did you mean?"

He raised an eyebrow and his eyes skimmed her body from boots to hat. When he was done with his slow perusal, every inch of her skin burned. She felt herself blushing and wanted to look away, but her pride wouldn't let her. Instead she lifted her chin and held his gaze.

"I think you know, but just in case I wasn't clear, I was talking about you, Audrey. You are definitely the most beautiful sight in this place and I can't stop looking at you."

Her breath caught in her throat and her heart thudded in her chest. She couldn't let her emotions get the better of her common sense. "Are you trying to get inside my head? Is this some sort of game?"

She hoped he was being sincere, but the wary part of her refused to take his words at face value. After all, the Battle of the Sexes started tomorrow. He might be trying to get an edge.

"No game. I'm just being honest. I should be concentrating on the competition, but instead I can't stop looking at you. Can't stop thinking about you."

"So you're going to blame me for your poor performance?" She was definitely going to blame him if she didn't ride as fast and as cleanly as she normally did. But she wasn't going to let him know how often he was on her mind. Heck, he had made himself at home, moving in furniture and setting up housekeeping. But that was her little secret. He might be in a mood to share, but she wasn't.

He shook his head. "I can't win. I was trying to pay you a compliment. That's all."

Regret turned her stomach. She hadn't meant to offend him. There was no reason she should have been so harsh with him. And, truthfully, she was normally so much better at recognizing and receiving compliments. But being around Jack scattered her good sense.

He started to turn to walk away.

"Wait," Audrey called.

He paused, one eyebrow raised.

"Sorry. I'm generally not so—" she flapped her arms uselessly "—something."

"Apology accepted. I forgive you for being so…something."

Despite herself, she giggled.

"But what makes you think I'm going to have a poor performance? I was off my game yesterday, but I'm back, baby." He flashed a bright smile that sent shivers dancing down her spine.

"Well then, there's nothing to say to that."

They stood there, staring at each other. There was very little space between them, but neither of them moved away. He reached out and tucked a stray hair behind her ear. His hand brushed against her cheek and her heart fluttered and her knees weakened at his touch. It took supreme effort to not lean into his hand and prolong the contact. To not turn and brush her lips against his palm. Audrey searched for something to say, but nothing came to mind. The silence stretched between them until her horse neighed, shaking her out of her stupor.

"I need to finish up here," she said, even though she had already done everything she'd intended to do.

"Then I'll leave you to it." He tipped his hat and strode away. And though she ordered herself not to stare, she couldn't pull her eyes away for a million dollars. There was just something so appealing about him. From his muscular back to his firm backside and strong thighs, he was truly a sight to behold. She didn't breathe normally until he'd turned the corner, disappearing from her sight.

She leaned against LemonDrop and whispered, "Just between you and me, I'm falling for that guy and I don't know how to stop."

Chapter Eleven

Audrey stood in the corner of the auditorium, hidden in the shadows, as she watched Jack compete. She'd redeemed herself today by coming in first in the barrel-racing event, making it easier for her to enjoy Jack's performance. She held her breath as he rode into the ring on a bucking bareback bronc. Audrey was impressed by his skill and when his eight seconds were over, the crowd rose as one in a standing ovation. In a moment she realized she was cheering and applauding along with everyone else.

Jack jumped off the back of the bronc and waved his hat in the air as he acknowledged the crowd. Then he was gone and she was left in awe. There was no doubt in her mind that he had won the event.

"Pretty impressive."

Audrey turned and looked into Remi's smiling face. "I never said he wasn't good. He's one of the best. I just wish he was as willing to acknowledge our skills."

"I understand that. He might just need time to see the light."

"Maybe. But I'm not going to wait around while he does."

"Corinne is going out with Mike," Remi said, smoothly changing the subject. "Brynn and I are going to get something to eat and then take in a movie. Maybe do a little shopping. Do you want to join us?"

Audrey shook her head. She enjoyed her sisters' company, but she wanted some time alone. "No. Thanks. I'm going to grab something to eat from one of the vendors and walk around for a while."

Remi gave Audrey a quick hug. "Okay. We'll see you at home."

Audrey nodded. After her sister walked away, she wandered around the conference center. Once she'd finished competing, she'd changed into her street clothes, so she was able to blend in with the crowd. She grabbed a hot dog and a frozen lemonade and went outside.

"Hey."

She turned at Jack's voice. Despite her vow to get her feelings under control, her knees wobbled a bit as his baritone reverberated through her. "Hey yourself."

"Are you waiting for your sisters?"

"No. Corinne is hanging out with Mike, and Remi and Brynn went out to eat and to the movies. I wanted to be alone so I decided to hang around here. What about you? I know where Mike is, but where's Ross?"

"He's meeting up with some friends from high school."

She nodded.

"You mentioned wanting to be alone. If I'm getting in the way of that plan, I can leave."

She didn't even have to consider that offer for more than a moment. Solitude lost its appeal when there was an option of being with him. Her hand on his arm stalled him. "You're not bothering me. I was just going to walk around town for a while. You can keep me company if you want."

"I want. Where were you planning on going?"

"I hadn't decided yet. I love every part of this town so much. It might sound a little bit weird to you, but it feels kind of like it's hugging me. You know what I mean?" She glanced at him at the risk of seeing a smirk on his face. She was relieved when he only nodded.

"Bronco is a special place. I enjoy life on the circuit. And, not to sound like Dorothy in *The Wizard of Oz*, but there really is no place like home."

She felt a twinge of envy and fought it back. She'd spent so much of her life on the rodeo circuit that she didn't consider anyplace home. But she didn't want to be the type of person who begrudged others things she'd lacked. Besides, she had a good life. She had wonderful parents and the best sisters anyone could ever want.

After a brief discussion, they decided to go downtown. Truthfully, Audrey would have been happy going to the garbage dump. She really wanted them to get along again. She missed their easy rapport and wished they could go back to the way they'd been. When they'd parked their cars and were strolling down Main Street, each drinking a milkshake they'd gotten from Bronco Java and Juice, she decided to take the big step and make her feelings known.

"Jack, this is really nice."

"The milkshake?"

"Us getting along. All the hoopla surrounding the Battle of the Sexes might not bother you, but it's really starting to wear on me. Maybe it comes from being a middle child, but I like for everyone to get along. The stress of this war between us isn't doing my peace of mind any favors. So I'd like to call a truce."

He laughed and she wanted to punch him. She was being open and had made herself vulnerable, and he thought it was funny? "I'm a middle child, too, which might also account for my desire for peace."

She blew out a breath, relieved that she hadn't given in to the urge to slug him. She probably would have just hurt her hand anyway. His muscles were rock-hard. She held out a hand. "Friends?"

He gave her hand a firm shake. "Friends."

"Since we're friends and all again, I have to be honest."

"Uh-oh. Does that mean you're about to lay into me?"

This time she was the one who laughed. "Not at all."

"That's good to know. Then, please, tell me whatever you want. It won't go any further than here."

"I hope not. But who knows? Perhaps instead of just being followed and photographed, maybe someone is bugging our conversations."

"I think we're safe from that."

She did, too. "I know. I have to tell you that I'm a bit tired of everything."

"What 'everything'?"

"This." She gestured between the two of them. "This Rodeo Sweethearts stuff. I feel like Chuck and the organizers just pushed us together, hoping that we'd hit it off. To tell you the truth, I'm feeling a bit exploited."

"In what way?"

"They're using this supposed romance between us to sell tickets to their Battle of the Sexes exhibition. It's affecting my performance. Today's barrel racing aside, I am so much better than how I've performed."

He nodded. "I know. I looked you up the other day. And to be honest, I'm better than what I've done. We both were back on track today, though."

"That's true. But it took supreme concentration and effort. Plus, LemonDrop is a superior horse. We've competed together for a while and she really knows the job."

He was silent but she could see from the expression on his face that he was truly listening to what she was saying. He was taking her words to heart, which she appreciated. It made her next confession that much easier to make.

"Jack, I'm thinking about quitting the Bronco rodeo and letting my sisters compete without me."

"What?"

"I feel like I'm letting them down."

"Letting them down? How?"

"It's different for you and your brothers. You each have your own reputations. Sure, you compete in some of the same rodeos, but you guys also go your separate ways. And even when you do compete at the same rodeos, your scores are your own. They don't reflect on Mike or Ross or Geoff. It's different for me. My sisters and I are a unit. We're billed as the Hawkins *Sisters*. What one does affects all of us, and our reputation as a whole. And it's not just us four. Don't forget, we're the second generation to compete as the Hawkins Sisters. If I fail, it's a reflection on my mother and my aunts. Heck, it even affects my grandmother."

He put his hands on her shoulders and leaned down so their eyes met. His eyes bored into hers. "Stop. Inhale." When she just looked at him, he gave her a gentle shake and repeated his order. "Inhale."

She sucked in a deep breath.

"Now exhale."

She complied.

"Good. Now let's find somewhere to talk." He looked around. There was a bench not far away, so he led her there.

After they'd sat down, he turned to her. "That's a lot of weight you're toting around. It has to be heavy, especially for someone so small."

She knew he was only trying to lighten the mood, but she couldn't crack even the slightest smile.

"Anyway," he added, "I can't tell you how to feel, but I can tell you how it looks to an outsider."

Audrey steeled herself and then nodded for him to go ahead.

"I think you're doing great. Better than great. You honor your mother and aunts with every performance. I can't imagine them feeling anything other than pride in you. I bet if you asked your sisters, they would tell you the same thing."

Her heart swelled with his every word until it was near to bursting and she could only whisper. "Thank you."

"And, true, my brothers and I don't compete as a team, but you had better know that Ross, Mike and I feel the responsibility to live up to the Burris name, both in and out of the arena. Geoff has set a high bar."

"One that you intend to surpass," she guessed. It didn't take a genius to see that Jack both admired his brother and wanted to exceed his incredible achievements.

"It's that obvious, huh?"

"Maybe just to me. Let's face it, you and I are both really competitive, more so than our siblings, Geoff excluded."

"Agreed. At least when it comes to Ross and Mike. It's a toss-up between Geoff and me."

She laughed.

"And as far as being exploited, I understand

how you feel. I feel the same thing, although maybe not as deeply as you. I understand the need to sell tickets. And the Rodeo Sweethearts are definitely a draw."

"But Mike and Corinne are the real deal. They're actually dating. So why aren't they the face of the competition instead of us?"

"I couldn't tell you. Maybe because I'm so much better-looking than my brother."

She poked him in the chest, impressed by the muscles she felt. "Be serious."

"You think I'm kidding?"

"I think you're vain." She'd agreed with his assessment, but she wasn't going to let him know that. His ego was already too big.

"Back to you quitting. I don't think you should."

"I don't want to. I want to wipe up the floor with you."

He laughed. "Well, that's not going to happen, but everyone needs a goal."

She crossed her arms over her chest, noticing that his eyes followed the movement. "So what do you suggest? I don't want to keep going on this way. Fighting is taking the fun out of everything."

"Well, we do have another option."

"I'm listening."

"Since we're sharing, I want to apologize."

She touched his hand. "Apologize? For what?"

"I know I'm at least partly responsible for the

tension you're feeling. I'm the one who wanted us to stop seeing each other, ending our friendship."

"Yes. You said it was the professional thing to do, as if I were an amateur who didn't know what it took to have a great competition." Of course, since she hadn't performed her best the first day, he might have been onto something. Not that she would ever admit that to him. Wild horses wouldn't drag it out of her.

"Is that what you thought? I wasn't questioning your professionalism. I know you're a pro. The truth is, that was just an excuse on my part. You were taking up a lot of my thoughts and I needed to focus. I thought keeping my distance would help with that."

"Oh." She smiled.

"And as you can tell, it didn't. So, I'm thinking about our options. Chuck and the promoters might have done everything in their power to push us together and make it seem like we're having this great romance, but they weren't wrong about everything."

"They weren't?" Her voice squeaked but he didn't seem to notice.

"No. There's something real between us." He cleared his throat and then speared her with his eyes. "Maybe we should stop fighting it and see where things go."

"Oh."

He leaned closer and then cupped her face. "What do you think about that?"

With him this close and his scent wrapping around her like a comfortable blanket, it took monumental effort to think, but somehow she managed long enough to reply. "I like the idea."

"I was hoping you would." His face was only a few inches away from hers. He smiled wickedly before he brushed his lips across hers. The contact was brief, but it was electric, sending shocks throughout her body. She wouldn't go so far as to say it was life-altering, but she knew that she would never be entirely the same.

Jack pulled back and then looked around. She realized they were in the middle of downtown and quickly did the same. There were several people around, but nobody appeared to be paying that much attention to them. Considering the fact that they'd been photographed in an alley where they should have been alone, she didn't take much comfort in that. It only took a second to take a picture with a camera phone. Heck, someone could have been videoing their entire conversation and they'd been too involved to notice.

He evidently felt the same way. "We should probably go somewhere private to…continue this conversation."

"Where do you suggest?" she asked.

"I'm staying with my parents. It's never been

an issue before, but now…" He winced and shook his head.

"You feel like you're sneaking a girl into your room?"

He nodded. "Sad but true."

"No worries. My sisters won't be home for hours."

"That's good to know."

He stood and held out his hand. Without the slightest hesitation, she took it and let him lead her to the lot where they'd parked. When they'd left the convention center, she hadn't been assured that they would be getting along at the end of the night, so she'd driven. That way, if things had taken a turn for the unpleasant, she wouldn't have been dependent upon him for a ride back to her vehicle.

When they reached their cars, she pressed the key fob, unlocking her car. He reached out and she thought he was opening the door for her. Instead he held it closed. She looked at him, silently questioning his action.

"I might be living dangerously here, given the number of times that we've been photographed unaware, but hey, I'm a cowboy. Taking risks is in my nature."

"What?"

"There is no way that I'm going to be able to drive all the way to your house without kissing you. And that little peck back there on the bench doesn't count."

"Is that right?" She leaned close to him, pressing her breasts against his hard chest. His eyes narrowed and he sucked in a breath and wrapped his arms around her waist. She had intended to tease him, but from the serious expression on his face and the heat suddenly burning between them, she'd been playing with fire.

"Yeah. That's right," he replied. And then he was kissing her. Their lips parted and his tongue swept inside her mouth. It was nothing like the sweet, tentative kiss they'd shared a little while ago. This was so much hotter. And much more demanding. His touch scorched her and heated her insides, turning her blood into molten lava. There was no way she was going to be satisfied with only a kiss, no matter how hot the kiss was. She wanted more. Needed more.

Her knees gave way and she leaned against him for support. After a moment, he started to pull away and she tightened her arms around his neck, holding him in place. He lingered a minute longer and then ended the kiss. She moaned in disappointment and felt his laughter against her lips.

"I hate to be the one to spoil the party, but we don't want to attract more attention than we have. I'm holding onto my control by a thread.

There are things that I want to do that we can't do in public. At least not without risking an indecency charge."

She stiffened and tried to retreat to create a proper distance between them. But she was pressed against her car door, so there was nowhere for her to go.

As if realizing she was suddenly uncomfortable, he moved a few steps back.

"Thank you." She ran a hand through her hair and then looked at him. She could read the caution on his face. She touched his jaw, hoping that one act would convey her emotions. She hadn't changed her mind about being with him tonight. But she wanted to maintain as much privacy as they could—however little that might turn out to be.

"I'll follow you."

"Okay."

He opened her car door and held it for her.

After she'd started the motor, he climbed into his car. As she drove down the street, one thought kept circling her mind. She and Jack were about to take a big step in their relationship. Despite all that had occurred between them, she believed it was the right one.

Chapter Twelve

Audrey led Jack up the stairs to the second floor, holding her breath until they reached her bedroom. Knowing what they were about to do, envisioning them naked in each other's arms, she couldn't quell the excitement or the nerves that fluttered in her stomach.

As she stepped inside the room, she closed the door behind them and then crossed over to the bed and turned on a lamp on the nightstand. She looked at him and all nervousness fled. This was *Jack*. Despite all of the issues and misunderstandings of their past, she knew he was one of the good guys. He was a man she could trust. She smiled at him.

"I suppose I should join you over there," he said.

"That would be nice."

In the blink of an eye, he was beside her. He took her in his arms and kissed her. The kiss started out sweet, but the fire between them flared to life, engulfing them.

"You smell so good," he murmured against her neck.

The feel of his lips on her skin turned her bones to liquid and she leaned against him for support. "You feel good. And you're making me feel good."

"Baby, you haven't felt anything yet. Let me show you how good you can feel."

He undid the first button on her shirt. His hand brushed against her breast, his caress promising pleasure to come.

One by one, he undid the buttons and anticipation stole her breath. When he slid the shirt from her shoulders, she stood proudly as he stared at her body, appreciation in his eyes.

"My turn," she said, reaching for him.

He spread his arms in surrender. "I'm all yours."

She held his gaze as she undid his buttons. Although her fingers trembled, she didn't look away. Neither did he and they communicated their unspoken feelings with their eyes.

When she was done, she pushed the sleeves

off his shoulders, down his arms, and he let his shirt fall to the floor.

Her eyes moved to his bare chest, taking in every inch. It was perfectly sculpted, and she reached out and caressed him. His skin was smooth and warm.

He sucked in a breath and his eyes darkened. Without looking away, he unbuckled his belt while she unfastened her jeans. Once they'd shed their clothes, they fell into the bed. His arms wrapped around her, at once arousing and reassuring. With each caress, her feelings for him grew along with her yearning.

Although they were competitors in the ring, they weren't battling now. By silent agreement, nothing in the outside world was allowed to intrude on this moment. They were completely in sync, each giving and taking pleasure. But this was more than simply physical. With each caress, each kiss, they were making an emotional connection that wouldn't be easy to break. Audrey was opening her heart to Jack and it wouldn't be easy to close again when they were no longer in this sanctuary.

"Wow," she breathed sometime later as she wiped a hand across her damp brow. There was so much she wanted to say, but somehow nothing she thought of would adequately express the depth of the emotions she was feeling. Not when her body was still humming from Jack's touch.

He kissed her bare shoulder. "You can say that again."

"Wow," she said and then laughed. She felt so at ease with him and loved that they could laugh and joke minutes after they'd just made love for the first time. The fact that they would be competing against each other tomorrow didn't seem an insurmountable problem. Of course, she still intended to beat him so bad that he cried for his mama, but for the first time since it was introduced, she saw the competition as something separate from their relationship. Thank goodness he'd talked her out of quitting. "Making love with you is a five-star event. I definitely recommend."

"Only five stars?" He leaned on one elbow and looked down at where she lay on her pillow. Grinning devilishly, he dragged a finger across her lips. "I definitely need a second chance so I can get a better rating."

"Just what number are you looking for?"

"How many stars are there in the sky?"

"Oh."

He lowered his head to kiss her. Her stomach growled and he paused and shook his head. "You cannot possibly be hungry."

"Why not? I haven't eaten in hours. Besides, I just burned a lot of calories." She draped an arm over his neck, pulling him closer. "I'm sure I can wait a few minutes."

He kissed her. "I can get behind that plan."

Her stomach growled again and he pulled back. "How about we get something to eat?"

She laughed. "I guess you'll have to improve your rating later."

"Count on it." His expression was serious and her heart sped up in anticipation.

They took a quick shower together and then dressed and went into the kitchen. She pulled open the refrigerator. "What would you like?"

"What do you have?"

"Cheese, chicken breasts, ground beef, veggies. Eggs. You know, the usual stuff one has in a refrigerator."

"Not everyone. My refrigerator is where leftover takeout goes to die."

She shook her head. "How about I make a stir-fry? It's quick and easy."

"Sounds good. What can I do to help?"

She rubbed her hands together. "Oh, an eager assistant. How about you help chop the vegetables? Starting with the onion and garlic."

"I can do that."

Audrey grabbed tomatoes, mushrooms, carrots and peppers from the vegetable drawer and quickly washed them. She gave Jack a knife and he got to work chopping.

After putting a pot of rice on to cook, she began slicing the chicken into bite-size squares. She heated oil in a pan and then added the garlic Jack had chopped for her. The aroma filled the air, making her taste buds water. She added the chicken chunks so they could brown, stirring them occasionally to keep them from sticking.

"You're pretty handy with that knife," she said. Jack had finished with the onion and was now slicing the tomatoes.

"My mother insisted that my brothers and I know how to handle ourselves in the kitchen. She made sure that we can cook a few dishes so we won't starve."

"But I thought you said you couldn't cook."

"No. You assumed that's what I meant. I can cook. I just don't have a lot of time to do so. You know how hectic and draining life on the road can be. I don't want to spend what little free time I have grocery shopping and cooking. It's easier to grab food somewhere."

"I enjoy cooking. I find it relaxing."

"To each his own, I suppose."

Audrey turned down the flame under the rice and then added the vegetables to the chicken. She whipped up a sauce and poured it over everything. A few minutes later they were seated at the kitchen table. She looked at Jack. "Give it a try."

"It smells so good, I know it's going to be delicious."

She waited until he'd taken a bite. "Well?"

He nodded and sank his fork back into his food. "Even better than it smells. You are a wonderful cook."

"Thanks." She picked up her fork and began to eat as well. They talked nonstop while they ate. They were polishing off seconds when she heard the front door open.

"We're back," Brynn called, walking through the house.

Before Audrey could reply, she heard Remi shush their sister. "Didn't you see Jack's car outside? They might be asleep or otherwise occupied."

Audrey felt her cheeks grow hot as she looked over at Jack. If he was embarrassed by Remi's comment, it didn't show.

Jack reached out and touched her hand. "I see your sisters are as perceptive and annoying as my brothers."

That comment made her laugh. "Yep."

Brynn and Remi stepped into the kitchen.

"Hey, you two," Remi said, smiling.

Brynn nodded her greeting. No doubt she was slipping into mother hen mode. She clearly hadn't made up her mind how she felt about Jack. But then, since his and Audrey's relationship had been a rocky affair, that was understandable.

"Hi." Jack's smile encompassed both her sisters.

"We aren't interrupting anything, are we?" Remi's eyes danced with delight. She was all-romance, all the time, so naturally she was beyond pleased to see them together.

"Nope." Jack glanced at his watch and then stood. "But it's getting late, so I should get going."

"Don't let us run you out," Brynn said.

"You aren't. I need to get my rest if I'm going to compete at my best tomorrow."

Audrey stood and avoided looking directly at her sisters. As the oldest, Brynn had a highly developed sixth sense and could read her sisters like books. "I'll see you out."

As they walked to the front door, Audrey was acutely aware of everything about Jack. The intimacy they had shared earlier in the evening was in the forefront of her mind. Not just the physical closeness, although that had been amazing, but the emotional closeness as well. After an initial struggle, she'd felt comfortable sharing her innermost thoughts and feelings with him. It was never easy for her to be vulnerable with many people, but Jack had made it feel as natural as talking with her sisters.

"I had a good time," he said when they were

alone on her front porch. The sun had long since set and the sky was a dark blanket with shining stars only beginning to pop out. The streetlights provided some illumination, but she and Jack were in the shadows, giving the illusion of being the only two people in the world. That, given the fact that her sisters were inside the house, was pretty fanciful, even for her.

"So did I."

"Now, about tomorrow…"

"If you're going to ask me to go easy on you because you rocked my world, forget about it. I still intend to beat the pants off you."

He laughed. The sound was so free it reached inside her. "That's my girl. So sure of herself. I'll use those words for motivation. So remember you said them when I come in first and you're a way, way, way distant second."

"You talk a lot of trash. But then you've only seen me when I've been off my game. But I'm back. And let me tell you, you ain't seen nothing like me before."

He put his hands on her shoulders and he grew serious. "That's what I want to hear. I'll see you tomorrow. And, truly, I wish you the best of luck."

"You should keep that luck. You're going to need it a whole lot more than I will."

He shook his head and kissed her lips, fast and hard, leaving her lips tingling. Then he turned and jogged down the stairs. Fingers pressed to her mouth, she watched him drive away. Her legs were still weak from the kiss and as she recalled the way he'd made love to her, she wobbled. Hopefully she would be fully recovered by tomorrow. She would need to be her best if she intended to back up her bold words—which, of course, she did.

"So, you and Jack," Brynn said as soon as Audrey returned to the kitchen. Her sisters had cleared the table and were washing the dishes.

"I was going to get those," she said.

"Don't try to change the subject," Brynn said.

"I wasn't."

"I thought you didn't want to hang out with us because you wanted to spend some time alone. Clearly, you left off the part about Jack being part of that alone."

"How was it?" Remi asked before Audrey could explain what happened.

"How was what?" Audrey answered.

"Don't play games," Brynn said.

Audrey smiled and sank into a chair. "Wonderful. It was wonderful."

Her sisters exchanged smiles and then joined her at the table.

"That's good to know," Brynn said. "But was it good enough to knock you out of your funk?"

"I wasn't in a funk."

"No? Then what was it that had you doing so poorly?"

"I was in a slump that was totally unrelated to Jack." That sounded so pathetic that when her sisters laughed, she couldn't help but join in.

"Do you think he might be the one?" Remi asked.

"Good grief, girl, slow down," Brynn said. "It was only one time and you've already got her married off."

Audrey was too startled to say anything. She believed that there was a special someone for everyone. But could Jack be the one for her? She didn't know. And right now she didn't want to think that far down the road. Because, as close as they'd been tonight, there was still the competition between them.

One thing she knew for sure, Jack was proud. He wanted to be Cowboy of the Year. There was no way his ego could handle being beaten by a woman. That was too bad because she intended to beat him tomorrow. And that might spell the end of their relationship before it got started.

Jack whistled as he walked into the house. His parents were sitting together on the sofa, watching a romantic comedy. Jack knew for a fact that his father preferred sports and documentaries. But for as long as Jack could remember, his father watched whichever movie his mother wanted to see without complaint. He might occasionally yawn and once, he'd even fallen asleep, but for the most part, he endured.

"That's love," his father had explained when Jack had asked him why he watched those movies. "Sometimes you have to do what makes your woman happy even if it's something you don't want to do. And you know she does the same for me. Do you really think she wants to go to all of those basketball tournaments?"

Jack enjoyed his life on the road, but he really missed the love his parents showered on him whenever he came home. It felt good to be back, even if only for a short while. He sat in a chair and watched the tail end of the movie with them.

"That was good," his mother said, turning off the television.

"I thought so, too," Benjamin said with a grin.

"You are so lying," she said and then kissed him. "But I love you, so I'll forgive the dishonesty."

Jack laughed. His parents' relationship made him believe in true love. He wondered what it felt like to love someone enough that you'd willingly watch romantic comedies. He immediately thought of Audrey. His feelings for her were different than those he'd felt for any other woman he'd ever been involved with. Stronger. Just what was he willing to sacrifice for her?

"I'm going to bed now," Jeanne said. "I have my Zumba class in the morning and I'm going to need all of my energy."

"Good night," Jack said.

"What's wrong?" Benjamin asked when they were alone.

"What makes you think something's wrong?" Jack asked instead of answering.

"Oh, let's see. I'm the father of four sons and I know each of you. I always know when something is bothering you. But the fact that you sat here and willingly watched the last fifteen minutes of that chick flick is a dead giveaway."

"True."

"Besides. You have a tell. If I had to guess, I'd say it's a woman problem. Something to do with that Hawkins young lady that you're seeing. Am I right?"

Jack chuckled. His father never ceased to amaze him. He wondered if he would be as perceptive when he had children. Not that he was contemplating such an idea at his age. There were still too many things he needed to accomplish before he would even think about settling down with a woman, much less having children.

"You still have skills, I'll give you that. I would

think they'd be rusty since we haven't lived here for years."

"Don't forget, I'm a high school principal and basketball coach. I deal with dozens of kids every day. So spill."

"You're right. It's Audrey. I'm falling for her, but there's this whole rodeo thing. The organizers came up with this Battle of the Sexes idea. It would be bad enough if it was just our family versus theirs, but Audrey and I have that head-to-head competition tomorrow."

"I hear the event is sold out."

"Yeah. But the problem is the competition."

Benjamin rubbed his chin, a sign that he was paying close attention. It also meant that he wasn't going to interrupt Jack with questions or comments.

Jack appreciated that his father was a good listener, but Jack knew that he was going to have to spill his guts if he wanted his father's advice.

"I really care about Audrey and I know it would mean a lot to her to win, but I don't want to lose to her."

"That wouldn't be good for the Cowboy of the Year competition. And it wouldn't do your image any favors either."

"No." He was leading in the race for the honor, with Geoff only a few points behind. But there were no points involved in the Battle of the Sexes. "I know I can beat her."

"Then what's the problem?"

"I told you. She wants to win. Audrey wants to show people that women belong in rodeo and that they're just as good as men."

"Maybe she's right."

"Rodeo is dangerous for women. And Audrey is so small."

"You're thinking about Janet."

Jack nodded. "She was my friend. I like to think she still is. I call her every week, but she still won't speak to me. Yesterday I called her mother's number, but she made an excuse as to why Janet couldn't talk to me. I knew it wasn't true. She was trying to get me off the phone. Janet and I were so close. I just don't understand why she kicked me out of her life."

"Perhaps it's because you remind her of everything she's lost. She's trying to accept her new reality and get on with her life. You need to let her do that. When she's ready to talk to you again, she'll call you. But don't lose sight of the fact that what happened to her was a tragic accident. It doesn't mean rodeo is any more dangerous for women than it is for men."

"Maybe. But men are stronger."

"You're forgetting that men have been injured and even killed in rodeo, too."

Jack knew that. He also knew that was why his parents had worried so much when each of their four sons had decided that they wanted to make a career in rodeo. His parents had wanted them to go to college and then get good, safe careers. Eventually, Mike and Ross would be leaving the rodeo to pursue other careers. But Jack? Rodeo was in his blood. He couldn't imagine doing anything else in the foreseeable future. Sure, he knew that his body would eventually make competing difficult, but that time was far from now. He was just beginning to see the fruits of his labor paying off, finally winning and getting the recognition he'd always wanted.

"I haven't forgotten about the danger. But that's not the problem."

"Then what is?"

"Everything else aside, I actually wouldn't mind losing to her if she was better than I am. But she's not. Yet, since I know how much it means to her to win, I'm actually considering throwing the event. I wouldn't do it in an obvious way. Maybe by a second here or there."

"I see. Then what's the problem?"

"That seems disrespectful to me. I'd never consider letting a man win. And if she figured out what I was doing, she would give me hell. Audrey might be small, but believe me, she's nobody's pushover."

"Well, it seems to me that you have your answer."

"I do?" He must have missed that part of the conversation.

"Yes. Do your best and may the best competitor win."

"I know. But..."

"But what?"

"She's going to be hurt when I beat her, and the thought of hurting her—" He shook his head. The thought of seeing her in pain made it hard to breathe. He didn't think his heart could bear her disappointment.

"Is too painful to handle?"

"Exactly." He blew out his breath. "So what should I do?"

His father grimaced and then patted him on the shoulder. "Your guess is as good as mine. But I have confidence that you'll figure it out. Whatever you decide, I know it will be the right thing."

"I hope you're right."

They rose and went to their bedrooms.

When Jack lay in his bed, he recalled holding Audrey in his arms earlier that evening. He worried that after the competition tomorrow he wouldn't have that chance again.

And that thought was the most painful of all.

Chapter Thirteen

Audrey stood near her sisters, trying to gain control over her emotions. She was normally not nervous before the start of a rodeo, but this was something different and her stomach churned. This time she was competing directly against Jack, proving that men and women were equals and should be treated as such. But if she were honest, it was more than that thought that caused her nerves. It was thoughts about Jack.

Last night had been as unexpected as it had been wonderful. Of all the things she had imagined taking place with Jack, making love hadn't been one of them. But when they'd kissed and he'd held her in his arms, it had felt so right. So natural. She'd let her emotions run free and she had simply followed where they'd led her. And they had led her to heaven, or as close as one could get while remaining on earth.

But now she was about to compete against him, and she needed to get her head back in the game. She couldn't let herself forget that this was much more than a simple battle between the two of them. There was more on the line than coming out on top. Her victory would prove that women and men could compete as equals and should be given equal opportunities. Equal publicity and support. And most of all, equal prize money.

"Ready?" Brynn asked.

Audrey nodded. She and Brynn were competing together in the team roping event. Although today was all about the exhibition between Jack and Audrey, the organizers had thought it would be good to include one team event to showcase the two families' skills.

"Yes."

Audrey and Brynn got on their horses, which were in side-by-side pens with a steer penned in between. There would be two rounds to this event. Audrey would be the header for the first round while Brynn was the heeler. They would switch positions for the second round.

Audrey backed her horse into the corner and

nodded that she was ready. The steer was released, and it began running toward the center of the arena. Audrey waited until it had gotten the appropriate head start and then she kicked LemonDrop into action. Her horse charged into the arena behind the steer and Audrey took aim. She threw her rope and it wrapped around the horns, and just as quickly she spun the steer around so Brynn could rope the back legs. The crowd roared and she looked at the clock to check their time. Five point three five seconds. She and Brynn exchanged grins as they rode back to the pens. They had tied their best score of the season.

After dismounting and handing over the reins to rodeo helpers, Audrey and Brynn went to watch Jack and Ross compete. Ross was header for this round and Jack was the heeler. They roped the steer in five point six five seconds. Audrey whooped and she and Brynn hugged each other. They were leading by three-tenths of a point. Audrey had always known they were just as good as the men. Now the rest of the world would know it, too.

She and Brynn returned to the pens for the second round. This time Brynn was the header and Audrey was the heeler. They ended up with a time of five point six five seconds, exactly what Jack and Ross had received in their first round. Audrey was a bit disappointed with their time, but it was consistent with the times they generally received when she was a heeler and Brynn was the header.

Audrey watched nervously while Jack and Ross prepared to take their turn. Even though she knew she should be focusing on her next event, she couldn't keep her eyes off Jack. He looked so gorgeous in his blue shirt, faded jeans and his customary black cowboy hat. He wasn't dressed any differently than any other cowboy on the circuit, yet he stood out. He looked so good, he should be on the cover of a rodeo magazine so all of the world could have the pleasure of looking at him.

She watched as the steer ran through the ring, followed closely behind by Jack, who was the header this time. He expertly roped the horns and then Ross just as expertly roped the rear legs. Audrey's eyes immediately flew to the clock. Five point three five seconds. Unbelievable. The exact time she and Brynn had received on their first round. Disbelief soon gave way to disappointment. They were tied.

Brynn was thrilled by the result and Audrey forced herself to smile. Her resolve to beat Jack wasn't going according to her plan. But there were still the individual events. She would just have to beat him there.

There was a brief break in the action so she

and Jack could rest and prepare for the next event. Her sisters surrounded her, congratulating her and Brynn and encouraging Audrey for the barrel racing. Of all of the events, barrel racing was her least favorite. Even so, she was among the top-rated riders in the country, and knew that she had an advantage over Jack in this event. Cowboys didn't barrel race, and although Jack hadn't done so since junior rodeo, he'd been willing to accept the challenge.

When it was time to ride, her sisters hugged her.

"Good luck," Brynn whispered.

Jack's brothers had been talking to him as well, but after wishing him good luck, they left the area. Audrey couldn't help but notice that Mike and Corinne were side by side, laughing as they went. Clearly, the two of them weren't taking the competition nearly as seriously as she and Jack were. Even so, she was going to have a conversation with her baby sister to remind her of where her loyalties were supposed to lie.

"So much for family loyalty," Jack muttered.

Audrey laughed as she looked over at him. "I was just thinking the same thing."

"At least you and I have our priorities straight," Jack said with a grin.

"You'd better know it," Audrey said. But when he smiled at her like that, it took great effort to set their personal relationship aside and remember that they were on opposing sides in this competition.

She mounted LemonDrop and when the whistle blew, she and her horse charged down the alley toward the first barrel. LemonDrop might only be four years old, but she was well trained. And fast. In addition to speed, barrel racing required horses to be agile. Audrey trusted LemonDrop to know exactly what to do, so she let her horse have her head.

When they reached the first barrel, LemonDrop sped around it and then headed for the second barrel and finally the third. Once they'd circled all three barrels, LemonDrop turned and flew back to the alley. Audrey checked the clock for her time. Seventeen point seven two seconds. She seriously doubted that Jack could beat that time.

She had barely dismounted when Jack went flying by on his horse. Audrey watched from the side as he flew through the arena, his horse kicking up dirt. He finished with a time of nineteen point eight one seconds. She'd beaten him and was now leading! She reminded herself that gloating was unattractive, but she couldn't keep the broad grin off her face.

But there was very little time to enjoy her lead. She had to get herself ready for the calf-roping event. She and Jack didn't speak during the break in the action, each choosing to keep focused on what was important.

Winning.

Audrey's heart was pounding in her throat as she mounted her horse and waited until the calf had been released from the pen. When it passed the barrier, she took off on her horse, her rope in her hand. She threw it and it landed around the calf. She released the rope and checked her time. One point eight seven seconds. No way Jack was going to beat that.

Audrey crossed her fingers as Jack took his turn. When he'd roped the calf, she glanced at the clock and let out a loud whoop. His score was one point nine seconds. She'd beat him.

That left the final competition—bareback bronc riding. Audrey was really psyched for this event. She enjoyed bareback riding. It was her very best event and she currently led all the cowgirls on the circuit. The problem was, Jack was *excellent* at it. She was just going to have to do better than she had in the past if she was going to hold on to her slim lead.

Unlike the timed events, bronc riding was a judged event. The rider needed to stay on the bronc's back for eight seconds to earn any points. The bronc could potentially earn fifty points, depending on bucking and spinning, and the rider could also earn fifty points, for a total of one hundred.

She'd drawn a really rank bronc, but she had ridden tough broncs in the past. She nodded her head and the gate swung open. Women were allowed to use both hands in this event, but for this ride Audrey was determined to ride with one hand, as Jack would be required to do. She didn't want anyone to say she had been graded on a curve.

Time seemed to move slowly as the bronc bucked back and forth and then around. Audrey held on to the rope with one hand and kept the other in the air so she wouldn't touch by accident. Her internal clock ticked away each second. Then the buzzer sounded and she released the rope and jumped from the bronc's back.

She ran over to the fence encircling the arena and jumped on the bottom rung, grabbed her hat from her head and waved it back and forth to the roaring crowd. The ovation was the loudest and longest of her life. She would never forget this moment.

She jumped down from the gate and returned to the backstage area. Remi and Corinne hugged her.

"Are you out of your mind?" Brynn yelled furiously. "Why did you ride with one hand? You could have been hurt. Or worse."

"I can ride as well as any man. I don't need two hands."

"Oh, yes, you do. And if you ever pull a stunt like that again, you'll be sorry. You'll be out of the Hawkins Sisters so fast your head will spin." Brynn leaned down so that her eyes met Audrey's. They flared with anger. "No more dangerous stunts. Got me?"

Audrey had never seen her sister so furious. Hopefully she never would again. The bravado drained from her, and Audrey nodded. And though she hated to admit it, Brynn was right. That had been a risky thing to do. "Yes."

Jack had been in the pen across from her, setting up on his bronc. She turned her attention to the arena just as he began his ride. Time slowed as she watched him. Her heart was in her throat as the bronc tossed him around, and she could barely breathe as she waited for his ride to be over. Finally, the buzzer rang and he hopped from the bronc's back and acknowledged the cheering crowd.

Jack stood still and listened as the spectators roared his name. He had never been in front of such a raucous crowd before, at least not one that was chanting his name. In the past, he'd stood in the shadows, watching as Geoff's performance was rewarded with cheers. It felt good to be the recipient of such adoration.

He was the first to admit that his admiration for his brother had a bit of envy mingled within it. Not that he believed Geoff hadn't earned his accolades. Jack had witnessed firsthand the hours upon hours of practice Geoff put in. And Jack had been the recipient of his brother's advice and wisdom, whether it be tips to improve his performance or information about the tendencies of various broncs and bulls. Still, it felt good to be the one in the spotlight.

This had been one of the hardest rides of his life. Not because of the bronc. But because he'd been competing against a very determined Audrey. His heart had nearly stopped when he'd seen her bronc riding with one hand as the men did. He'd had flashbacks of watching Janet be horribly injured in an accident. There was no way he would have survived if Audrey had been hurt.

Thankfully she hadn't been. His fury with her for taking such an unnecessary risk had morphed into pride at her successful ride. That pride had been replaced by a determination to best her. She'd shown the crowd what she could do. Then it had been his turn to let them see Jack Burris at his best. And he had. They'd appreciated his skill. Hopefully the judges would, too.

Finally, the cheers died down and Jack returned backstage. He looked around for Audrey. When he spotted her, he walked straight over to her. Despite the fact that there were cameras all around filming their every move, he pulled her into his arms and held her tight. She wrapped her arms around his waist and leaned her head against his chest.

"This has been some competition," Jack said.

"Yes. No matter how it ends, I know that I've done my best."

"Your best is pretty darn good," Jack replied. "I was so impressed by you, Audrey. You are one heck of a cowgirl."

Audrey smiled and he knew she heard the sincerity in his words. Then he gave her a gentle shake. "Why did you ride that way? One-handed?"

"Because if we're going head-to-head, we should use the same rules. When I win, I don't want to hear you crying how you would have won if you could have used both hands or if I'd only used one."

"You should know me better than that by now."

"Meaning what? That you wouldn't have used that as an excuse?"

"Not that. I'm not going to lose. And the only person who's going to be crying is you."

She laughed and poked him in the side. "Keep telling yourself that, cowboy."

"Seriously, though. You did really well, Audrey. No matter the outcome, you've opened a lot of eyes with your performance." Including his. He couldn't believe he'd actually assumed she and her sisters were gaining so many fans because of their looks and glamorous outfits. All of the interviews he'd seen had focused on their beauty with limited—if any—discussion about their skill. He should have known there was more to them than their appearance. Thank goodness he'd never said those words to her and she'd never know what he'd once thought.

"You really mean that," she said. Although she'd spoken softly, he heard the emotion in her voice.

"I do."

"Thank you. You'll never know how much that means to me."

Before he could assure her that he did, a volunteer approached them, bringing the intimate moment to an end.

"Sorry to interrupt. They want you in the arena for the announcement of the winner. Good luck to both of you."

"Thank you," Jack and Audrey said in unison before walking side by side into the ring.

"Well, that was some competition. Now all we need to do is find out who is the winner," the announcer said.

Jack felt Audrey stiffen beside him and a part of him hoped that she would win. But since that meant he would lose, he shoved that thought aside. Instead, he hoped that they would be judged fairly and that they would each accept the results with good humor.

"I know you're all waiting for the results of the head-to-head competition between our Rodeo Sweethearts. They put on a good show, didn't they? Put your hands together for them one more time."

The crowd roared again as Jack and Audrey stepped back into the spotlight. The acknowledgment felt good, but the tension was getting to him.

"But before we announce the winner, I want to introduce a special guest who's here in the arena today."

Jack tamped down his impatience.

The announcer continued. "Let's give a Bronco welcome to our own Geoff Burris."

Jack sucked in a breath as he watched his brother jog to the center of the arena. When had he gotten to town? He hadn't been at their parents' house last night or this morning. But then, Geoff's fiancée had her own place, so he'd probably spent the night there. For a brief moment, Jack felt a bit of jealousy as the spotlight went from him to Geoff. But then he glanced down at Audrey. She was looking at him as if he were the only man in the arena. Her admiration meant more to him than the applause of a hundred crowds.

Geoff waved to the audience and then stepped out of the spotlight and went to stand in the shadows.

The announcer then got on with the program. "And the winner of the Battle of the Sexes between Jack Burris and Audrey Hawkins is…" He drew out the moment, looked at a piece of paper he held and then laughed. "You are not going to believe this, but the judges have checked and rechecked their scores. It's a tie."

Jack and Audrey looked at each other. He held his breath as he waited for her reaction. Would she be disappointed that she hadn't won? Then she smiled at him, and he sighed with relief. A tie was the perfect way to end the competition and the best thing for their relationship. Since neither of them had lost, they each could walk away with their pride intact.

They accepted the trophy and held it between them. Then they turned and walked around the arena so that fans could take pictures of them, accepting the many congratulations that came their way.

Once they stepped out of the arena, they were immediately swarmed by reporters who wanted to interview the "Rodeo Sweethearts." There were a good number of reporters surrounding

Geoff, too, but that was fine by Jack. In the past, he might have thought Geoff was stealing his thunder, but with Audrey by his side, he knew he had been the ultimate winner.

"The two of you had been doing a bit of sparring on social media. How does it feel to tie?" a local reporter asked, shoving a microphone into Jack's face. This was the third time he'd been asked some variation of that question.

"It feels great," he answered honestly, as he had every other time. "Audrey is a great competitor. Very skilled. She deserved to win just as much as I did. And as you can tell, the judges felt the same."

"Given your relationship, did it feel strange to compete against Jack?" the reporter asked Audrey.

"Not at all," she replied. "We're professionals and we're able to keep our personal lives separate from our business lives."

"So there is something personal going on between the two of you. Do you care to elaborate, Jack?"

Audrey flashed him a slightly panicked look. They'd been speaking to reporters for a while and each time he'd believed they were done, someone else asked a question. He could tell she was getting tired of the numerous questions, especially the ones about their private lives.

"Not at the moment. Audrey and I appreciate your attention and congratulations. But I would like a moment to speak with my brother. Thanks again, and talk to you later."

"Thank you," Audrey said and then backed away from the press. When they were at a safe distance, she looked at him. "This is something else. Generally, only one or two reporters bother to interview us. And even then they only ask one or two questions. I haven't been bombarded like this before."

"I tried to end the interviews a few times, but they didn't seem to get the hint. I hope the personal questions didn't upset you."

"No. But to be honest, I would have preferred a few more questions about what life is like as a woman on the rodeo circuit and fewer fluff questions."

"You mean you didn't want to talk about how you keep your hair so lovely under your hat?"

She laughed. "Not even close to what I want to discuss."

"But it is lovely. In fact, all of you is glamorous." He had been joking, but suddenly he became serious. "You really are beautiful, Audrey."

Her laughter fled and she looked at him shyly. A flash interrupted them, and he looked around. Someone was filming them from the distance.

This very public arena was the last place they should be having a private conversation.

She stepped back. "I need to get going. You go catch up with your brother. I'll see you tomorrow for the Hawkins Sisters versus the Burris Brothers."

He hated the idea of not seeing her until tomorrow, but before he could try to convince her to spend more time with him today, she'd walked away.

Sighing, he sought out Geoff. He hadn't had the opportunity to really talk to him in a while—a telephone conversation where Jack vented about the Hawkins Sisters and the Battle of the Sexes not withstanding—and he relished the opportunity.

Geoff was finishing an interview and Jack stood back, waiting until the last question had been asked and answered and the reporter had walked away before approaching his brother.

"Hey, man," he said, giving Geoff a big hug. "It's good to see you. Why didn't you tell me you were going to be in town?"

"It was a last-minute thing. Besides, it felt good to watch from the stands. You were darn good today."

His older brother's praise warmed his heart. He'd always had a bit of hero worship, as most younger brothers did for their older brothers. He still did. "Thanks."

"It looks like you got on board with the Battle of the Sexes after all."

"Yes. It turned out to be more fun than I'd thought."

"And of course there's your relationship with Audrey."

Jack smiled at the mention of Audrey. They'd grown closer during the event, and even though they hadn't said the words, he knew their relationship had changed after they'd made love. He wished they'd had time to talk about their feelings. There was so much he wanted to tell her.

"There's that," he agreed.

"Is it serious?"

"Why are you asking me that?" Although he was close to his brother, Jack didn't feel comfortable discussing his feelings for Audrey with him. She deserved to be the first person to know how he felt.

"Because I'm your big brother and I'm concerned about you. One minute you're telling me and anyone who'll listen that the Hawkins Sisters are a novelty act that you wished had never come to town. And you certainly didn't believe any of them was a worthy competitor. Then, a few days ago, I started seeing pictures of you and Audrey all over the place. You're blowing up social media, and those gossip magazines and celebrity TV shows are talking about the 'Rodeo Sweethearts' every day. Not that I give any credence to any of that. I remember what they did to me and Stephanie. Even so, the photos tell quite the story. I'm concerned. You've had a pretty big change of heart in a short period of time. So, tell me, are you in love with Audrey?"

Jack's pulse raced and he froze. Was he in love with Audrey? Was that why he always wanted to be around her and why her happiness mattered so much to him? He knew his feelings were deeper than respect and concern, but love? He didn't know. But he certainly wasn't going to tell his brother that before he was sure. And even then, he needed to let Audrey know how he felt first and then discover if she felt the same. The thought that she might not love him was like a dagger in his heart, stealing his breath.

"Well?" Geoff prompted when Jack only stood there lost in his thoughts.

"Audrey and I just met."

"You need to be careful and take things slowly."

"I know you didn't just say that to me." Suddenly, Jack was angry, although he wasn't sure why. Perhaps it was the blatant hypocrisy. "Aren't you the one who fell in love with your fiancée in less than a month?"

"That's totally different. I knew Stephanie was the one for me the moment I laid eyes on her."

"If I recall correctly, you were on pain medications and nearly delirious at the time. You thought she was an angel."

"She is. *My* angel."

Jack rolled his eyes and started to walk away.

"Listen," Geoff said, grabbing Jack by the arm. "All I'm saying is that you need to be careful. Before you met her, you weren't impressed by her or her sisters. You called them all glitter and no substance. A joke. Or have you forgotten saying that?"

Of course he hadn't forgotten. He couldn't believe he'd been so blind. He could only comfort himself with the knowledge that no matter how angry Audrey had made him, he'd never insulted her with those words.

"No answer?"

Jack spun around at the sound of Audrey's voice. The pain he heard there was nearly enough to rip out his heart. Then he looked at her face. Although her expression was filled with fury, her eyes told another story. She was devastated. Because of him.

"Audrey." He quickly closed the distance between them. He reached out for her hands and she jerked away.

"Is it true? Did you really say that my sisters and I are a joke?"

"I can explain."

"So you did say it." The agony in her voice wrecked him. How could he have been such a fool?

"If you would just listen to me. Please, give me five minutes."

"Listen while you make up a lie? I don't think so. I'm glad you had some fun at my expense. How you must have laughed. You were so convincing earlier. And to think, I was starting to…" She shook her head.

"Please. Let's go someplace where we can talk privately," Jack begged. "I can straighten this all out."

She swiped a hand across her cheek and he realized that she was crying. His proud Audrey, who hated to show weakness, was so badly hurt that she couldn't hold back her tears. Tears that he'd caused. "There's nothing more to say. Nothing will ever change what you said. You're a jerk, Jack Burris, and I never want to see you again."

She turned on her heel and then stalked away.

He closed his eyes and his head dropped. He knew without a doubt how he felt. He loved Audrey. And he'd lost her.

Chapter Fourteen

"I want to tell you again how sorry I am," Geoff said the next day as he and Jack walked into the arena. He'd apologized for the situation with Audrey numerous times since the blowup. He'd even offered to talk to Audrey on Jack's behalf, but Jack had turned him down. He didn't need his big brother's help. This was Jack's mess and he needed to clean it up.

"It's not your fault," Jack said. The blame lay squarely on Jack's shoulders. He was the one who had hurt Audrey. The words she'd overheard had actually come out of his mouth. There had been a time when he'd thought the Hawkins Sisters were a novelty act and that women didn't belong in rodeo. He'd believed it was too dangerous. But that was before he'd gotten to see them compete. Before he'd seen just how skilled they were and how hard they worked to perfect their craft. True, he'd died a thousand deaths as he'd watched Audrey ride that bronc with one hand yesterday, but if anything, it had proved that she was just as skilled as any man competing in rodeo today. Maybe more so.

"Still, I should have kept out of it. I don't know why I butted in like that, sticking my nose where it didn't belong. I guess I just fell back into big brother mode."

"That's easy to do." Jack himself had been guilty of it from time to time with Mike and Ross, so he knew it could happen. Besides, it didn't make sense to brand Geoff the scapegoat for his own idiocy. Somehow, someway, he was going to convince Audrey of just how sorry he was. That was, if he could get her to listen to him, something that was still uncertain.

He'd called her as soon as he'd gotten home yesterday, but his call had gone straight to her voicemail. He'd let an hour pass before he'd tried again. He had hoped that she'd had time to calm down in the interim and that she'd be willing to hear him out. He was willing to grovel, beg, and cry if necessary. He would let her rant and rage at him if she'd only pick up the phone.

A part of him had hoped she'd told her sisters what had happened, and that Remi or Corinne would convince her to give him a chance to explain. After all, they seemed to like him. But that call and the subsequent ones he'd made had gone unanswered.

He'd briefly considered going to her house to see if she would speak with him, but if she wouldn't answer the phone, there was less chance she would open the door to him. After calling her five times, he'd realized he was being a nuisance. The last thing he wanted was to come across as desperate. No, that wasn't true. He was desperate and he didn't care if she knew it. But he didn't want her to think that he was going to turn into some stalker ex-boyfriend that she needed to fear.

With each passing hour, the hope that she'd eventually give him a chance to explain diminished. He wondered if she would even show up at the convention center today. After all, there were four Hawkins sisters and three Burris brothers in the Battle of the Sexes. If she pulled out, her sisters could still compete.

That thought wrecked him. He knew how enthused she'd been about the event. Showing the world what she and her sisters could do animated her. The idea that he had stolen some of her joy made his heart ache.

He hurried into the backstage area of the arena, not breathing an easy breath until he saw Audrey. She was dressed in faded jeans that hugged her bottom and a red silk shirt covered with patches of her sponsors. The blouse fit snuggly across her breasts, and not for the first time, he noticed just how sexy she was.

He looked into her face. Their eyes met and hers narrowed. When she didn't walk away, he took that as a positive sign. Maybe she was willing to listen to his explanation and accept his apology. Of course, it could just as easily be her way of letting him know that she wasn't going to run away from him. He didn't see any sign of fatigue on her face, which was a huge relief. The idea that she'd spent the night tossing and turning in her bed, as he'd done, didn't sit right with him. She hadn't done anything wrong.

This might be the only chance he got to speak with her, so he inhaled deeply and crossed the room. She lifted her chin but otherwise stood unmoving until he was mere inches away from her. The urge to caress her sweet jaw was tempting and he fisted his hands. Realizing that his stance could be misinterpreted as confrontational, he forced his fingers loose and then shoved his hands into his pockets. "Hi."

She simply stared at him. Okay. Did he really think it was going to be that easy? When had anything with Audrey been anything other than hard? But then, he didn't deserve easy.

His stomach had never lurched this way, even when he'd sat on the back of a bronc for the first time. He smiled, trying to mask his nerves, and started over.

"I'm glad to see you here. For a minute I worried that you weren't going to show up."

"Really?" Her sexy lips curled in a sarcastic smile, and he knew he'd stepped in it. "Despite what you obviously believe of me, I'm a professional. I made a commitment to compete in this Battle of the Sexes and that is exactly what I intend to do. Now, if you'll excuse me, I need to find some glitter and sequins so I can dazzle the audience. Hopefully they'll be so distracted by my sex appeal that they won't notice my lack of talent."

"I never said you weren't talented," he said.

"Whatever." Muttering under her breath, Audrey stormed away, joining her sisters, who were gathered near the pens. He glanced at them and her sisters shot daggers at him with their eyes. He'd expected Brynn to be cold to him—he'd never believed he'd entirely convinced her that he was one of the good guys—but he was thoroughly shocked by Corinne's and Remi's expressions. They looked like they wanted to toss him into the nearest pile of dung and bury him there. If they'd been rooting for a romance between him and Audrey, it was safe to say he'd ruined that. He no longer had a friend among the Hawkins sisters, so he could give up his hope of them pleading his case with Audrey.

He decided to get out while he still could, seeking out his brothers. When he reached the men's dressing room, Mike snatched his arm and glared at him.

"What's wrong with you?" Jack asked, yanking his arm away. With the disastrous status of his relationship with Audrey, he was in no mood to deal with his little brother's antics.

"You." Mike shoved him hard and he stumbled into a wall.

"Are you nuts?" He shook his head and then stalked over to Mike and got in his face.

Ross had been reclining in a chair and watching a video on his phone. He jumped to his feet and got between them. "Knock it off, you two."

Jack straightened his shirt and blew out a breath. He needed to calm down before things got out of hand. He took a step away from Mike.

"He started it," Mike said angrily.

"I started what?" Jack said. "I have no idea what you're talking about."

"I'm talking about you and your chauvinistic attitude. You calling the Hawkins Sisters a sideshow. All glitter and no substance. I heard all about it from Corinne. She's pissed and has the mistaken idea that because we're brothers we think the same way."

"I—"

"Not to mention that you've hurt Audrey's feelings," Mike said, talking over Jack. "They think you were playing with her emotions. Now, because of her loyalty to her sister, Corinne won't speak to me."

"I'm sorry. I didn't mean for any of this to affect you."

"Who the hell cares what you meant? You messed this up. Now you had better fix it. And fast." Mike poked Jack in the chest and then stalked away before Jack could tell him that he'd tried but Audrey wasn't having it.

Given Mike's current state of mind, that was probably for the best. This behavior was totally out of character for him. Mike was usually so easygoing and forgiving. For his brother to be this upset over Corinne... Whew.

Jack wasn't giving up on setting things right with Audrey. Not by a long shot. But he couldn't exactly toss her over his shoulder, carry her away to a secluded location, tie her down and make her listen to him. She'd claw his eyes out if he tried.

The image of carrying Audrey on his shoulder

brought back memories of the fun they'd had at the photo shoot. Had that only been a couple of weeks ago? So much had happened since then. His feelings had grown so much stronger. Deeper. He wasn't going to let Audrey walk out of his life without a fight. There had to be a way he could win her back. But first there was the Battle of the Sexes to get through.

The event today would go much the same way that it had yesterday with the exception that the participants wouldn't be limited to him and Audrey. Thank goodness. The last thing their relationship needed was head-to-head competition. No matter how upset he was with the dismal state of his relationship with Audrey, and now the tension between him and his baby brother, Jack needed to stay focused on his job. Being distracted for even a split second could lead to disastrous results, or worse yet, an injury. Besides, if he didn't give a peak performance, Audrey would accuse him of throwing the event because he didn't think she and her sisters were worthy competitors. And if he and his brothers beat them as they no doubt would? The situation wouldn't improve then either. This really was the worst of all worlds.

Who would have thought one exhibition could have such a big impact on so many relationships? There was no time to think about it any longer, thank goodness. The entire depressing situation was giving him a headache.

Jack and Mike were up first in team roping. Mike would be the header for the first round while Jack was the heeler. Mike glared at him as he mounted his horse. Although they were in separate pens, the heat from Mike's stare practically singed Jack's skin. Mike clearly cared about Corinne and the brothers' relationship wasn't going to be repaired until Jack straightened out things with Audrey. Jack couldn't really blame Mike for being upset. He would be furious if some jerk had caused a rift between him and Audrey. Unfortunately, some jerk had. *Jack.*

The gate swung open and the steer raced into the arena. Although Mike and Jack weren't in sync personally, they worked perfectly as a team, roping the steer in only a few seconds. Once they would have congratulated each other on their time. Not now. Mike joined Ross as they prepared to watch Remi and Corinne compete. Jack thought it was wise to give his brother some distance, so he stood alone and watched.

The sisters made a good team although they were nearly a second behind Jack and Mike's score. They seemed happy with the results, though, which he supposed was all that mattered.

Then it was time for Brynn and Audrey to compete. Jack's breath stalled in his chest as he watched Audrey mount LemonDrop. He willed her to look in his direction, but she didn't. It was as if he'd ceased to exist for her.

The steer was released and he watched in awe as Audrey and Brynn worked in tandem to rope it. Without looking at the clock, he knew that they'd bested his and Mike's score. No doubt about it. This time a tie wouldn't satisfy her. Audrey was in it to win it.

They finished the timed events with Jack and his brothers holding a slim lead. With only two one-hundredths of a second separating them, the competition could go either way. But now it was time for the rough stock events. All three Burris brothers and all four Hawkins sisters would be competing in the bareback bronc and saddle bronc riding.

Jack tried not to worry, but he prayed Audrey didn't ride one-handed again. His nerves couldn't take it and his heart would be in his throat the entire eight seconds.

The crowd cheered loudly after each rider. Thankfully, Audrey rode in the traditional way, although he was just as nervous. In standard rodeos, the competitor's score was announced after the ride had been completed. The organizers had chosen to do it differently here. They'd decided that it would be more exciting to wait until everyone had ridden before announcing the scores. At the time the rules had been explained to him, Jack hadn't cared one way or the other. Now, though, it seemed too easy for the judges to mess with the scores in order to increase the tension. That thought only showed how paranoid he was becoming. It was only an exhibition. Even so, he wanted Audrey to get her due.

As he watched the others, Jack had been happy that they'd all done well. No one had been disqualified and everyone had stayed on their broncs. Even though his emotions were churning through him by the time it was his turn, he had one of his best rides.

When they'd completed the last event, the announcer called them all out into the center of the arena, where a makeshift stage had been erected. The Hawkins sisters stood together on the right and the Burris brothers stood on the left. The families smiled and waved at the audience, giving no hint of the tension between them.

"Well, that was quite the event," the emcee said. "And what an exciting way to close out the inaugural Bronco Summer Family Rodeo. Let's give another round of applause for our wonderful competitors. Not just today, but for the entire event." The crowd cheered and whistled. Once the applause died down, the emcee continued. "Before we get to the winners, I've been asked to announce that we have raised five thousand dollars for charity."

The audience erupted into applause again. At any other time, Jack would be thrilled with the announcement. Now he just wanted everything to hurry up and end so he could talk to Audrey.

"Now, back to the final score. I was just talking to the judges and the scores are just too tight to declare a winner. They were arguing among themselves. For a minute there, it looked like they might come to blows."

Jack shook his head. He didn't know where they'd found this guy, but he certainly had the gift of gab. And he also managed to create drama, something that the audience seemed to appreciate.

"So there's only one thing to do," the emcee continued. "The judges have decided to let the audience make the decision. You'll get to vote. No, we won't be passing out ballots. Your cheers will decide the winners."

Jack didn't know how he felt about that, but since nobody asked him, it didn't matter.

The announcer pointed to Audrey and her sisters. "Let's hear it if you think the Hawkins Sisters won."

The crowd cheered long and loud. When the noise died down, the announcer pointed to Jack and his brothers. "Let's hear it if you think the Burris brothers won." Again the crowd cheered long and loud. To Jack, it was a tie. He could live with that. Anything to get this moment over. It was torture being this close to Audrey and to not be able to touch her.

The announcer shook his head. "Well, folks, it's easy to see that you enjoyed both teams. But somebody has to be declared the winner. So let's try that again. If you think the Hawkins Sisters won, let's hear from you."

Once again the crowd cheered loudly.

"And now, if you think the Burris brothers won, let's hear from you."

The crowd cheered louder and longer than they had previously. They'd chosen the Burris brothers as the winners of the Battle of the Sexes. Jack had always loved winning. He'd thrived on it. Not this time. Not when the victory had come at the expense of someone he loved. Knowing that Audrey and her sisters had lost sapped all of the joy from the victory. He tried to meet Audrey's eyes to let her know that she was a winner to him, but she stared ahead stoically.

When the announcer grabbed him by the arm and shoved the microphone into his face, he knew it was time to turn on the charm and address the audience. He still had a job to do.

"Thank you so much for voting for us. It was a tight competition, and the Hawkins Sisters are great competitors. They gave us all that we could handle and then some. Congratulations, Brynn, Remi, Corinne and Audrey. I guess that home-field advantage really made the difference today."

The Hawkins sisters smiled politely and waved to the crowd before walking from the stage. Jack wanted to follow them and talk to Audrey. If she got away before he had a chance to tell her that he loved her, he might not get a second chance. But the emcee was asking him another long-winded question and he had no choice but to stand there. Jack had previously sought the spotlight, so he knew he shouldn't complain now. Even so, he needed to bring this to a close.

Jack tried several times to wrap up the interview, but the announcer didn't get the hint. Instead, he kept asking him and his brothers question after question. Finally, unwilling to waste another precious second, Jack took the microphone and thanked everyone for coming. Then while the announcer stood there sputtering, Jack handed back the microphone and jogged from the arena.

He looked around backstage, but the Hawkins sisters were nowhere to be found. His heart began to pound as he raced to the women's changing room, hoping against hope that they were in there. He knocked on the door. No answer. After a tense moment, he opened the door a few inches and called Audrey's name. No response. His heart was hovering in the vicinity of his toes as he stepped inside and looked around. The chairs and benches had been swept clean of boots and outfits. Nothing of the sisters remained.

He knew Audrey couldn't possibly be in the room, yet the stubborn hope clinging to him propelled him farther inside. He looked around, checking every nook and cranny, before he accepted the truth. Audrey was gone.

He sank into the nearest chair, unable to stand under the weight of his disappointment. Audrey had walked out without giving him the opportunity to explain. But he didn't blame her. She didn't owe him anything. After what she'd overheard, she must be hurting. Truthfully, in her situation, he would have done the same.

After a moment of indulging in unfamiliar self-pity, he jumped to his feet. He was down but not out. Yes, he made a mistake by not speaking up when he had the chance, and there was no changing that now. But he was going to find a way to win her back.

If only he knew what it was.

Audrey loaded the last box of her belongings into her car and closed the trunk. A tear threatened and she blinked it away. She'd shed her last tear over Jack Burris. He wasn't worth one more moment of her time. And he was certainly unworthy of her emotions. But she was sad over more than the demise of her relationship. Men had come and gone from her life before and no doubt would again. Especially if she didn't do a better job of choosing them.

But what really hurt was the disillusionment she couldn't shake. She'd thought she and Jack were friends. More than that, she'd believed him when he'd said he respected her skill as a cowgirl. She couldn't rid herself of the disappointment she'd felt when she realized she'd misjudged his character. It was devastating to know that he wasn't the man she had hoped he was. But that was only part of the reason she wanted to cry.

They were leaving Bronco and wouldn't be returning. Though she and her sisters had only rented the house for the duration of the rodeo, the finality of the move hit her hard.

In the short time that she'd lived here, she'd come to love this town. She'd felt more at home in Bronco than she had in any other place she'd ever lived or visited. She hadn't been the only one who'd felt the pull of Bronco. Her sisters had felt the same connection. They'd even considered making Bronco their home base. They wouldn't rent a house together, of course, since they all wanted their own spaces, but they would have lived in this town.

Jack had ruined all of that. Audrey didn't want to live in his hometown. She'd never get over him if she kept running into him at Doug's or DJ's Deluxe or if she spotted his sports car around town. Because he'd done more than break her heart. He'd hurt her pride. He'd made a fool of her—mocked her and her sisters. He'd disrespected the work of her mother, aunts and grandmother. Women who had been trailblazers on the rodeo circuit. That was unforgivable.

"You ready?" Remi asked, coming to stand beside Audrey. Remi had been designated by their sisters to make sure that Audrey didn't spiral into depression. Audrey had already told Brynn, the ultimate mother hen, that she was fine. It wasn't as if she and Jack had been madly in love.

"Yep." She looked at the house that had been her temporary home and then turned in a slow circle, taking her last look at the block. Even though she hadn't gotten to know the neighbors all that well, she'd enjoyed the quick conversations they'd had whenever she'd encountered one of them.

But there was no time to waste reminiscing. The Hawkins Sisters had been invited to compete in a rodeo one hundred and fifty miles from Bronco. It started in two days and they needed to get a move on. Unlike their stay here, they would be in and out of town in under a week, so they would be renting motel rooms.

Audrey hopped into her car and then started the engine. Each of her sisters had their own cars and they started a caravan to the highway. She loved her sisters and confided in them about most things, but she was glad to have this time alone where no one would notice the occasional tear sliding down her face.

When Audrey saw the sign for the motel, she breathed a loud sigh of relief. The drive had taken slightly over three hours, including a break for a quick burger at a fast-food joint, and she was ready to get from behind the wheel of her car. What she really wanted was a nap, but she and her sisters had already agreed that after they'd checked into the motel, they were going to go to the stables to check on their horses.

They'd been using the same service to transport their horses for years, and trusted the drivers, but it was always a good feeling to see for herself that LemonDrop was happy.

As she brushed her horse, she talked to her, telling her what a pretty girl she was. LemonDrop nickered in response. Audrey glanced at her sisters, who were enjoying their own reunions with their horses.

Time flew as she got LemonDrop settled for the night. Caring for her horse helped to keep her mind from straying to Jack. And if she did find her thoughts wandering in his direction, she snatched them back and reminded herself that he was out of her life for good. Sure, there was always the off chance that they'd bump into each other on the circuit, but since it hadn't happened in the past, she didn't expect it to happen in the future.

They stopped at a family restaurant before returning to the motel. Audrey would have preferred to grab something at a drive-thru, but her sisters had insisted on eating a leisurely meal.

Once their food was set in front of them, Audrey admitted that they were right. She couldn't let her disappointment with Jack affect her diet. And the meatloaf, mashed potatoes and gravy, and green beans was just what she needed. The sisters kept the conversation light. By unspoken agreement, no one mentioned Jack or Bronco. She appreciated their thoughtfulness, but not talking about him did little to ease the pain in her heart.

Hopefully time would take care of that. She just wondered how much time it would take before she could breathe again.

Chapter Fifteen

"They're gone," Mike said, stepping into the kitchen and glowering at Jack.

"I know." He'd finally broken down yesterday afternoon and gone by the house Audrey and her sisters had been renting. He'd raced up the stairs and had been standing on the porch, ringing the doorbell, when the real estate agent had gotten out of her car, a For Rent sign tucked under her arm. She'd asked him if he was interested in renting the house. When he'd explained that he'd been looking for the Hawkins sisters, she'd shoved the sign into the grass and explained that their lease had ended and that they had vacated the property.

Nothing had hurt more than knowing that Audrey had actually left town without saying goodbye. And she hadn't left a forwarding address. Surely, the last words she'd said to him couldn't possibly be the last words he would ever hear her say.

Now Mike was ranting at him. "It's all because of you. If you hadn't been such a jerk to Audrey, Corinne wouldn't have left town."

"Wrong," Jack said, unwilling to take the blame for that. "The agent said the lease had ended. They stayed as long as they'd intended to stay."

"That shows just how much you know. Or rather, how little. Corinne said that they were considering making Bronco their home base. They wanted to live here."

Jack hadn't known that. Audrey hadn't said a word to him about settling down in his hometown. Why had she kept him in the dark? Did that mean she hadn't cared as much about him as he cared about her? That couldn't be right. He might have been wrong about some things, but Audrey's feelings weren't among them. She cared about him. Perhaps she had intended to tell him but had changed her mind after overhearing his conversation with Geoff. He had too many questions and not enough answers. And now he was unlikely to get those answers.

"Well, maybe they still are planning to settle down here. Perhaps they're competing in another rodeo and plan to come back to town when they're done." Of course, if they'd decided to do that, wouldn't they have extended their lease?

Mike shook his head. "You ruined things between me and Corinne. I'm going to do everything in my power to get her back. And if you have a brain in that hard head of yours, you'll straighten things out with Audrey." Mike stormed from the room. A minute later, Jack heard the front door slam. After sitting there a moment, Jack rose and began washing his cereal bowl.

"What's the problem between you and Mike?" Jack turned at his mother's voice. She'd just gotten home from her Zumba class and was dressed in her workout clothes.

Jack sighed. His parents had always set really high standards and expected their children to live up to them. They were good, honest people, and they'd raised their sons to be the same. Jack knew his mother would be disappointed in him when he told her how he'd hurt Audrey. True, he hadn't intended to cause her pain, but the intent didn't matter. What mattered was the result. And what he planned to do about it.

"He's angry at me because Corinne has left town."

"She's a rodeo queen. They travel. He knows that."

"Well, he's also upset with me because she's no longer speaking to him."

She put her hand on her hip. "You're just going to tell me this story piecemeal, aren't you?"

He laughed wryly. He'd already disappointed Audrey. He couldn't disappoint his mother, too. "Actually, I'm trying not to tell you the story."

"Okay. But remember, when you want to talk, I'm here. But I will say this before I let it drop. What happened between Mike and Corinne is between the two of them. They'll have to work it out themselves. Just as you'll have to work out things with Audrey."

"I made a mess of everything," he admitted.

"Then clean it up." His mother kissed his cheek and then walked away.

"I will." He just wished it were that simple.

Needing to get away from his thoughts, Jack hopped into his car. As he drove, he recalled the first time he'd let Audrey drive. That girl definitely had a lead foot. Speeding down the highway had been fun and he hadn't been able to keep his eyes off her. She'd been filled with joy. Her excitement had been contagious and he'd had more fun than he'd had in years.

When he reached downtown Bronco, he passed the street where they'd bumped into each other that fateful day. He slowed as he passed the alley where they'd gone to talk and had ended up kissing. He hadn't known it at the time, but that kiss had changed his life. Feeling her soft lips on his and holding her delicate curves pressed against his body had been heavenly. He might not have planned the kiss, but it had been inevitable. As inevitable as making love with her had been.

Thinking of the night they'd spent together made him realize just how much he had lost when he hadn't admitted to his brother that he was in love with Audrey. Perhaps he hadn't been sure at the time, but now there was no doubt in his mind. She was everything to him. Nothing mattered more than getting her back and showing her how much he loved her.

He drove aimlessly and ended up in front of Doug's. The bar was open, so he parked and went inside.

This was where it had all begun. The place where he'd first met Audrey. He stood inside the doorway and looked around. Instead of seeing the people sitting at the old, scarred tables, he pictured Audrey as she'd been that day. He could practically hear her joyous laughter floating over to him. The echoes were so real, she could have been there with her sisters. He glanced in that direction. Naturally, she wasn't there.

Instead, Winona Cobbs, an older woman in

town who claimed to have a bit of second sight, was sitting at the table. Rumor had it that she was somewhat of a matchmaker. His soon-to-be sister-in-law claimed that Winona had said that Geoff was the one for her before they'd even gone on their first date. In fact, Winona had known Geoff was Stephanie's patient even though he'd been admitted to the hospital under a fake name. Jack wasn't a believer in all that nonsense, but to each his own.

"Well, if you're going to stand there staring at me, you might as well buy me a drink," Winona said. "I seem to have come to the bottom of my glass."

Me? Jack mouthed, pointing at his chest and then looking around to be sure she was talking to him.

"Yes, you. You're staring at me so hard you're giving me a headache. If you keep it up, you're likely to drill a hole in my head." She used her foot to shove a chair away from the table, indicating that he should sit there.

What did he have to lose? He'd spent a lot of time thinking about Audrey and he hadn't come up with a way to clean up his mess. Maybe people were right about Winona, and she would have some insight. He crossed the room and sat in the chair she'd offered.

"How are you doing?" he asked politely.

She held up a hand, silencing him. When he only sat there looking at her, she chuckled. "And they claim old people are losing their memories." She held up her empty glass. "My drink."

"Right. Would you like anything to eat with that?"

"I could stand some fries. And maybe a cheeseburger with extra pickles on the side."

"That sounds good." He beckoned the waitress and placed Winona's order, getting the same for himself. They sat in silence until the waitress returned with their meals.

"So, you have women woes." Winona bit into her burger and then looked at him.

"Do I even want to know how you know that?"

She laughed. It was a robust sound that belied her skinny form. "What's to know? You've got a hangdog look on your face like you've lost your best friend. Pictures of you and that Hawkins girl were plastered all over town. I couldn't turn on my TV without seeing the two of you. If you were keeping your relationship a secret, you failed."

"Audrey," he supplied. Just saying her name sent a pang through his chest. Man, he missed her.

She grinned. "Yes. The Rodeo Sweethearts."

"The promoters came up with that name. Not us."

"Maybe. But it suited you. I saw the picture

of you kissing. I doubt if the promoters were behind that."

"No." That had been all him and Audrey and the emotions that had been running wild between them. The attraction had been too strong for either of them to resist for long.

"So, tell me what went so wrong that you wandered into a bar in the middle of the afternoon to drown your sorrows."

He thought about avoiding the question, but talking was definitely better than drinking himself silly. Especially since he knew he'd only end up with a headache to accompany his broken heart.

"I made a mess of things."

"So clean it up."

"That's exactly what my mother said."

"Wise woman. I always liked her." Winona grinned. "Always liked her sons, too. She and your father did a good job raising you and your brothers."

Ah. More of the Burris reputation to live up to.

"When Audrey and her sisters came to town, I wasn't very nice to her. In the past, I wasn't a big fan of women in the rodeo. I thought it was too dangerous for them. And I might have had a few chauvinistic ideas. I'm not too proud of that fact, but I've changed. But it's too late. I hurt Audrey. Not because of what I believed, but because of what I said about her and her sisters. And what I failed to say."

She nodded. "Hmm."

"So what should I do?"

She'd eaten while he'd bared his soul. Now she wiped her mouth and hands, swallowed the last of her drink and then stared into his eyes. "I told you. Clean up your mess."

"But how?"

"Truthfully, Jack. I have no idea. And what I think doesn't matter anyway. The answer to your problems is within you. You have to figure it out on your own."

She stood and he did as well.

"Thanks for lunch." She reached up and patted his cheek with her bony hand. "I expect an invitation to the wedding."

"You're awfully confident that things will work out."

"You want to be a champion, right, Jack?"

He didn't know what rodeo had to do with anything, but he nodded anyway. "Yes."

"Then you need to start acting like one."

That bit of advice given, Winona called goodbye to Doug and then walked out of the bar.

Jack sank back into his chair and pondered her words, trying to make sense of them.

Finally, it occurred to him that being a champion meant more than coming in with the best score in an event. It meant being Audrey's champion and championing her cause. That was the only way to win the prize that meant the most to him—her heart.

Jack paid for their lunches, left a substantial tip for the waitress and then left, feeling better than he had since Audrey had walked away from him without once looking back. He finally had a plan to win her back.

Jack took a deep breath and then slowly blew it out, ordering himself to relax. It wouldn't help his cause if he passed out in the middle of the interview. That would be newsworthy, but not the kind of news he'd planned to make.

After talking with Winona, he'd decided to do an interview to discuss women and rodeo. Specifically, he wanted to talk about the lack of respect the rodeo queens received. Since he had judged the Hawkins Sisters on their image, he had to come clean about himself as well.

During his travels, he'd encountered numerous other cowboys who had shared his chauvinistic attitude, so he knew it existed. Tonight wasn't about pointing fingers, and he wasn't there to judge. His goal tonight was to educate. If he could change just one cowboy's mind and make life better for even one rodeo queen, then it would be time well spent.

Of course, he hoped to reach more than one. But he wasn't naïve. He knew that even if he got people to think, it would take more than one conversation to change hearts and minds. He should know. It had taken losing the love of his life to really open his eyes.

Hopefully, after seeing this interview, Audrey would open her heart to him again.

She knew about the interview. Mike had reached out to Corinne and told her about it, and she'd promised to tell Audrey. That's all Jack knew about the relationship between Mike and Corinne. Jack hoped that they would work out their issues. It pained him to be the source of their problems. Maybe his words tonight would be what they needed to get back together.

"One minute," the stage assistant said to him.

"Thanks." Jack rubbed his hand down his white shirt and steadied himself. Then his name was called, and he went and sat across from the host. Although Jack preferred nature shows and documentaries, he watched his fair share of sports shows, including this one. Antonia, the host, was always fair to her guests, so he'd reached out to her to conduct the interview in the New York studios.

They made small talk, giving Jack time to get comfortable. Then Antonia smiled at him and got to the meat of the interview. "Your family is one of the most well-known in rodeo. Everyone knows your brother Geoff. But lately you've been making a name for yourself. You've had some big wins and you're in the lead for Cowboy of the Year. That must feel good."

"It does. I've worked hard and it's good to finally get the results."

"But that's not what you want to talk about. When you contacted the producers, you gave them a specific topic that you wanted to discuss. So why don't you tell us what it is?"

Jack had rehearsed for this moment several times over the past day. Now the time for truth had arrived.

"I want to talk about the changing face of rodeo. For so long, men have gotten all of the recognition and the praise and the biggest purses, while the women have had to settle for crumbs. Women work just as hard as the men do, often in half-filled stadiums. Men's events are nationally televised, while women's events go largely unnoticed. That's not fair to them. It's not fair to the public, who are missing out on seeing some great athletes."

"That's true. But it's the state of sports across the nation. Not just rodeo."

"I know. But the thing is, I don't have any influence in those other sports. I'm not sure how much influence I have in rodeo, to be honest.

But I know there are cowboys watching tonight. Many of them know me. They know I had some chauvinistic ideas. Not too long ago, I took a good hard look at myself. And I didn't like what I saw. I knew I could do better. That I had to do better. And I'm trying. I'm asking my fellow cowboys to change. I'm asking rodeo clowns, promoters and organizers to take a look at what we think about women in rodeo. Think about how we treat them. Let's treat them as the talented athletes they are. Let's give them the respect and recognition and pay they deserve."

Antonia nodded. "Well said, Jack. As a woman, I hope everyone takes your words to heart."

"I hope so, too."

"What brought about this about-face?"

"Personal experience. I recently participated in my hometown rodeo."

"The Bronco Family Summer Rodeo," Antonia supplied.

"Yes. And we were fortunate to have the Hawkins Sisters participate."

"For those of you who might not follow rodeo closely, the Hawkins Sisters are the granddaughters of legendary rodeo star Hattie Hawkins. Their mother, Josie, traveled the rodeo circuit with her three sisters as the Hawkins Sisters for years. They're retired now, and Brynn, Audrey,

Remi and Corinne picked up the mantle and they currently compete as the Hawkins Sisters."

Jack nodded. "That's correct. And it was the younger Hawkins sisters who competed in the Bronco rodeo. They were fantastic."

"Rumor has it that you and Audrey Hawkins were romantically involved. The press referred to the two of you as the Rodeo Sweethearts. Care to comment on that?"

Jack hesitated. Audrey hadn't liked people knowing about their personal life. Oh, she'd eventually begun to accept it, but she'd preferred not to have their relationship be the topic of conversation. She'd told him it made her feel exploited.

Any other time he would have given a meaningless response. But then, his reluctance to reply honestly to Geoff's question about his feelings was part of the reason for the demise of his relationship with Audrey. Not only that, he didn't have any other way of communicating with her. She wouldn't answer his calls and she ignored his texts. She'd even blocked him on social media. So he decided to go for broke. Besides, their relationship couldn't get any more over than it was now.

"That's true. The promoters thought that it would be good for the rodeo if people believed we were involved. But as time passed and we spent time together, the relationship became real. We fell in love."

"Really?"

"Yes. I can say unequivocally that I am in love with Audrey Hawkins. Sadly, I lost her. But I have no one to blame but myself. Audrey is one of the finest women—no, one of the finest people—I have ever met. She made my life better. Made me better. I've never been happier than I had been when we were together. But because of my chauvinistic beliefs—beliefs I no longer hold—I lost her.

"I know I don't deserve it, but I'm hoping Audrey will find it in her heart to forgive me and give me a second chance. I would do so much better." His voice cracked on the last words and his vision blurred. He blinked. He didn't want to break down on national television.

"Well, the romantic in me hopes things work out for you. Audrey, if you're watching, do me a favor. Have pity on this cowboy. Give him another chance." Antonia sounded sincere. Hopefully, if Jack's words alone hadn't convinced Audrey, the host's words would tip things in Jack's favor.

After the interview was over, they stood.

"I meant what I said. I hope things work out for you and Audrey."

"Thank you."

Jack walked away and went back to the airport. He could have spent the night in New York, but he wanted to get home. If Audrey had seen the interview and was considering giving him a second chance, he wanted to be as close to her as he could get.

"Come on, the show is about to start," Remi said, dragging Audrey into the front room.

"So what? You know I don't watch these sports shows. And when did you start watching them?" She looked around the motel room. Brynn and Corinne were there, too. None of them had ever wasted time watching sports shows. Why would they? The shows very rarely mentioned women's sports and they never paid attention to women's rodeo. She didn't believe in supporting people who wouldn't give her the time of day.

"This is different. Now sit down and watch," Brynn ordered.

"Just for a little while," Corinne said, flashing her sweetest smile, using all the baby-sister charm she could muster.

"Fine," Audrey huffed and then squeezed beside her sisters on the couch. She was trying to get comfortable when the show started. When the host mentioned Jack's name, Audrey jumped to her feet. "Oh, no. No way I want to look at this."

Brynn grabbed her arm and pulled her back down. "Just watch. If you don't like what he has to say, then you can forget about it. But maybe he'll say something you want to hear."

"Since when are you a member of the Jack Burris fan club?"

Brynn sniffed and brushed an invisible bit of lint from her blouse. "I'm not. But I remember how happy you were with him. And you've been miserable ever since we left Bronco. If Jack can say something to make you smile, I'm willing to listen. Aren't you?"

Audrey closed her eyes. She wanted to believe Jack would say something good, but she didn't want to get her hopes up only to have them dashed. But she was already hurt. She couldn't feel much worse than she did now.

"Fine. I'll listen. But I'm not promising anything. He's still a jerk who hurt my feelings."

"Agreed."

She couldn't stop staring at the TV screen. Jack looked gorgeous. His brown skin looked so rich against his white shirt. His chest muscles strained against the fabric, emphasizing what a perfect specimen of a man he was. She had caressed the chest. Been held in those strong arms. Been kissed by those lips. Been made love to thoroughly by that man. Her face heated as she recalled the blissful night they'd spent together.

As she listened to the conversation, the chains she'd locked around her heart began to loosen and eventually fall away. Breathing became easier. Each word he spoke, urging everyone associated with rodeo to respect the women of rodeo, was a soothing balm to her battered soul. When he admitted that he hadn't always done as he now preached, her anger lost some of its fire. He no longer believed that she and her sisters were all glitter and no substance, and regretted ever thinking that way.

She hadn't expected him to be this open and she was too stunned to do anything other than listen. When the reporter asked about their relationship, Audrey didn't know how to react. She didn't know if he had put their relationship behind them as she'd tried and failed to do. Would he say that? Or would he say that the Rodeo Sweethearts had simply been a creation of the promoters?

She held her breath as she listened to every word.

When Jack finished speaking, one thought repeated through her mind. *He said he's in love with me.* He hadn't whispered it in her ear, which would have been wonderful. No. He'd told everyone watching this nationally broadcast show how he felt. He loved her.

Time stood still as the words resonated in her soul. He loved her. She only became aware the interview was over when her sisters began talking at once.

Remi was clapping and laughing as if Jack had just proclaimed his love for *her*. Remi, with her romance-reading, rom-com-loving heart, was in her element. And though Audrey would never admit it to a soul, this did feel like a scene from one of Remi's favorite movies.

"I knew it," Corinne said gleefully. "I knew he was in love with you."

Audrey glanced at Brynn. Her big sister only smiled and asked, "So what are you going to do now?"

"Do?" Audrey asked.

"Brynn's right," Remi said, taking the reins of the conversation and running away with them. "After a romantic gesture like this, you need to do something equally romantic. It would be great if you could do a TV interview, too, but I don't know how long that would take. How about a TikTok video where you proclaim your love for him? Maybe in a song? Or we could recreate a scene from a movie? That shouldn't be hard to do. Or we can—"

"No, that's not at all what I meant," Brynn said, bursting Remi's bubble and hopefully halting her before she got carried even further away. Audrey wasn't interested in whatever harebrained scheme Remi was about to come up with.

"What did you mean?" Audrey asked. "I thought you were opposed to me and Jack being together."

Brynn shook her head, clearly aggravated.

"What I said was that you shouldn't chase him. I said you should be with someone who wants to be with you. Someone who appreciates you and values you as the wonderful woman that you are. I admit that, in the beginning, I wasn't sure Jack fit that description. But after the way he bared his soul in front of the entire nation, I think he does love you. And I have a feeling that you love him."

"Do you?" Corinne asked. "Do you love Jack?"

Audrey didn't hesitate. "Yes. I love him."

"Then I'll repeat. What are you going to do?"

"I'm going back to Bronco."

Chapter Sixteen

Jack stared at this phone and then paced from one end of the living room and back. He'd been checking it every few minutes ever since he'd done the interview three days ago. According to Mike, Corinne swore that Audrey had seen the interview. Jack had hoped that she'd been moved by his honesty and that she would reach out to him or at least unblock him on her social media. She'd done neither.

What did that mean? Was she still upset with him? Maybe she needed more time to process what he'd said. That was the best-case scenario. The worst case? She'd made up her mind that she was through with him and there was nothing he could do to change her mind. His heart sank at that thought. No. Despite the days passing without a word from her, he refused to accept that it was over. They hadn't known each other long, but he knew that she loved him just as he loved her.

And if he was wrong? Then what? He couldn't force her to love him. Love had to be given freely. And he definitely wouldn't stalk her. If she wanted him out of her life, he would go. But he needed to be sure she'd meant it when she'd said it was over and that it hadn't been her anger talking.

The problem was he had no idea where she was. He knew where she'd been. She and her sisters had competed at a rodeo about a week ago. He'd seen the scores online. His heart had swelled with pride when he saw that Audrey had won two events and come in second in another. He hoped her victories were a testament to her ability to compartmentalize and not proof that she was over him.

Jack knew all about compartmentalizing. At least he had until Audrey had burst into his life. Now no matter what he was doing, thoughts of her crept into his mind. Riding Spirit? Thinking of Audrey. Driving his car? Yep. Thinking about Audrey. Even though he knew it was impossible, he could smell her sweet perfume in the air. At times when he was overwhelmed with missing her, he wanted to cry.

He pulled out the picture that the photographer had given him. Now he could see the connection that others had seen when he'd been too clueless, too afraid, to recognize what had been in front of his face all along.

Audrey was perfect for him. She was the one he wanted by his side. But more than that, he wanted to be by her side as she faced life's challenges.

"What are you looking at?"

Jack jumped and turned at the sound of Ross's voice. It was a nice day, so he'd left the front door open and hadn't heard Mike and Ross come inside. "Nothing."

"It didn't look like nothing," Ross said, grabbing Jack's hand before he could slide the photograph into his pocket. "Aww. It's a picture of you and Audrey. How sweet. You're looking at her like she'd hung the moon and stars."

"Give it back," Jack said. He reached for the picture, but Ross held it away from him.

Jack wondered how much trouble he'd be in if he beat up his brother. They'd been raised not to fight with each other, but these were extenuating circumstances. He decided not to punch Ross in the nose, but only because he didn't want to risk getting blood on the picture. At the rate things were going, this might be the only thing he had left of Audrey.

"You haven't heard from her?" Mike asked, his voice dripping with sympathy.

Great. The only thing worse than being teased was being pitied. Now that Mike and Corinne were on speaking terms again, Mike had put his anger at Jack behind him.

"Would he be moping around if he had?" Ross said.

"I talked to Corinne like I said I would," Mike said.

"I believe you," Jack said.

"Maybe Audrey just needs time," Mike suggested.

"Or maybe she doesn't want to be with you anymore and she's hoping you'll get the hint," Ross said.

"What is wrong with you?" Mike asked, shoving Ross's shoulder.

"Nothing," Ross answered, giving Mike a shove of his own. "I just don't think pouring your heart out on TV and begging for a second chance makes a lot of sense."

"I suppose you think he should be more like you, the love-'em-and-leave-'em type."

"You don't see me crying over a woman."

"Your time will come," Mike said. "And when it does, I'm going to laugh my head off."

"No way. I'm sticking with my three-date rule."

"What's that?" Mike asked.

"Nobody gets one," Ross said and then laughed.

"You're a fool," Mike said, but he laughed, too.

Ross sobered and handed Jack the picture. "On a serious note, I'm sorry things didn't work out with Audrey. I liked her. And you were happy with her. Don't give up. Maybe things will work out for you like they did for Geoff and Stephanie."

Jack was moved by his brother's words even if he didn't think Ross meant them. Ross really didn't believe in true love. "I had hoped so. But maybe you're right. Maybe I have to accept that Audrey and I are done and move on."

"I never thought of you as the type to give up. Was I wrong?"

Jack spun around at the sound of Audrey's sweet voice. And there she was, standing in the middle of his parents' living room, looking like an angel. He would have thought he'd imagined her, but when his brothers greeted her, he knew she was real.

Jack wanted to speak—there were so many things he wanted to tell her—but all he could do was stare. He'd gotten used to seeing her dressed in jeans and boots. Today she'd swapped out her usual garb for a pink-and-purple floral dress that hit midthigh, showing off her sexy legs, and a pair of purple sandals. Her toenails were painted pink, which he found incredibly alluring. He could have stood there staring at her.

Ross nudged Jack's shoulder, pushing him out of his stupor. "Audrey. You're here."

"I knocked, but nobody answered. And the door was open so…"

"I guess we should leave you two alone," Mike said.

"Don't blow it," Ross whispered and then followed Mike out the door.

Once they were alone, Audrey gave him a pointed look. "You didn't answer my question."

What question? He quickly replayed everything she'd said. "No, you weren't wrong. I'm not the type to give up. But I am the type of man who respects a woman's right to say no."

"I appreciate that. And I did say no."

He nodded, trying to keep his disappointment to a minimum. Was she only here to tell him to his face that she wanted him to stay out of her life?

She smiled. "Tell me, do you respect a woman's right to say yes?"

"Uh, sure. I respect a woman's right to say anything."

"Then I'm saying yes."

"Yes to what?" Hope was trying to grow inside him, but he tamped it down. He needed to be sure first.

"Yes, to a relationship with you. Yes, to a second chance. That is, if the offer is still open."

Audrey blew out a breath as she waited for Jack to respond. Although she suspected that he would be agreeable to a second chance, she had walked in on him saying he would accept things being over between them, as if either way worked for him, so she was still a bit nervous. She should have called him to let him know how she felt after she'd seen the interview. That's what her sisters—even Brynn—had encouraged her to do. But she hadn't.

At first, she'd been too overwhelmed by her feelings to form a coherent thought. And later, she'd decided that she wanted to have the conversation face-to-face. That way they would be able to read body language as well as listen to words. She was coming to believe that a failure to communicate had been part of the problem between them. But she'd had commitments to fulfill and hadn't been able to get back to Bronco any sooner. Now, though, as she stood in front of Jack, waiting for his reply, she realized she shouldn't have let so much time pass without contacting him.

As she waited for his response, her eyes ate him up. Dressed in jeans and a designer shirt that must have been tailored to fit his body, he made her heart race. As usual, he was wearing one of the buckles he'd won in competition and clean cowboy boots. He was the most gorgeous man she'd ever seen. But more than being good-looking, he had a good heart. He might not get everything right, but he was willing to learn and improve. She couldn't ask for more than that.

"You already know the answer," he finally said. "It's yes."

She breathed a sigh of relief. While she'd been waiting, she'd been frozen in place. At his words, she was released. In less time than it took to exhale, she'd flown across the room and flung herself into his arms. He held her tight and she basked in the security of his arms. As the warmth from his body encircled her, she knew without a doubt that she never wanted to be anyplace other than with him. He was her home.

She eased back and looked into his face. Ever so slowly, he lowered his head and kissed her. When their lips met, electricity shot through her body. She could never get enough of kissing him. Gradually the kiss ended and Jack cupped her face with gentle hands. He looked at her, his eyes troubled, and her stomach tumbled to her toes. What could possibly be wrong?

He frowned. "I'm sorry for the way I answered Geoff's question. I should have told him how I felt about you. You deserved so much more than what I said. I also should have made it clear that

I no longer held those idiotic views about you and your sisters."

"Thank you for that. And while we're apologizing, I'm sorry for not giving you a chance to explain. I was hurt and angry, but even so, walking away was immature. You shouldn't have had to go on television to get my attention."

"I didn't mind doing the interview. The things I said about the way rodeo queens are treated needed to be said. I'm glad I had the opportunity to say them. Part of the reason I thought women didn't belong in rodeo was fear. My friend Janet was paralyzed in a barrel-racing accident."

"Oh, Jack. I'm sorry."

"So am I. The thought of another woman being hurt—*you* being hurt—is unbearable."

"I understand."

"I know you do. That's the kind of woman you are."

She smiled at the admiration in his voice.

"And I didn't mind telling the entire world how I feel about you. I'd do it again in a heartbeat. But now that you're here with me, I'll say the words to you directly."

Even though she knew what he was about to say, and he'd already said the words to the world, her heart sped up in anticipation. His recent actions had proved his feelings for her, but she longed to hear the words.

"I love you, Audrey. So much." His voice rang with sincerity.

She sighed. "I love you, too, Jack."

"That's the best thing I've heard in days."

He caressed her face. She wished they were alone and that she and her sisters had rented the house for longer. "Oh, by the way, I've decided to stay in Bronco."

"You have?"

She nodded. "It feels like home to me. The Hawkins Sisters have a lot of commitments. But when I'm not performing, I'm going to stay in Bronco."

"I like the sound of that."

"I'm glad. I'm moving back. Well, as soon as I find a place to stay."

"That won't be a problem. I can help you with that."

"You can?" She leaned in closer to him and sighed with contentment. All was right with the world.

"Yes. The house you and your sisters rented is still available. And from what I hear, the owner might be interested in selling to the right couple."

"Did you say 'couple'?"

"Yes. I know that we haven't known each other long, but I have never felt this way about a woman. And I know I'll never feel this way for anyone else. I don't want to rush you into anything. I should wait to propose to you in a way befitting a rodeo queen such as yourself, but I can't wait." He knelt and took her hand into his. The love she saw in his eyes was nearly her undoing. "I love you, Audrey Hawkins. Will you do me the honor of marrying me and making me the happiest man in the world?"

"Yes. Oh, yes."

Audrey stood by Jack's side as they looked at their families, who'd come together at the impromptu party to celebrate their engagement.

Once they'd decided that they wanted to spend the rest of their lives together, they had immediately called their family and friends, who'd been thrilled by the news. After seeing the two of them together and the photos that had been used in the campaign, their loved ones had suspected that there was something real between them. After Jack's open interview on television, everyone knew it would only be a matter of time before they reconciled. Nobody had been the least bit surprised when Audrey and Jack had announced their engagement.

Although they planned to have a more formal party in the future, they had wanted to host a gathering with their friends and family as soon as possible. Being new to town, Audrey hadn't known many places, but Jack had suggested The

Library, a restaurant owned by Bronco resident Camilla Sanchez. The building had actually once been Bronco's public library.

They hadn't rented out the entire restaurant since it was large enough to host their party as well as other patrons.

"Are you having a good time?" Jack asked right before he kissed her cheek.

"The best time ever. I'm so glad that my mother was able to come. She likes Bronco as much as my sisters and I do. She's even considering staying in town for a while." Josie was currently talking with Mike and Corinne. From the looks of things, Mike and Corinne had patched up their relationship.

"What about your father?"

Audrey shrugged. As far as she knew, nothing had changed between her parents. They were still separated. Her father hadn't been able to come to town on such short notice, but he'd wished her and Jack well and promised that nothing would keep him from walking his little girl down the aisle.

"I hope things work out for them."

"Me, too." She glanced over at his parents, who were surrounded by a small crowd of people. Benjamin and Jeanne had been very welcoming to her, claiming her as the daughter they'd never had. They'd also been very kind to her sisters, letting them know that they were always welcome in the Burris home. "Your parents seem to be having a good time."

"As always. They know just about everyone in this town. If someone grew up here, there's a good chance they were in my mother's kindergarten class or they went to high school where my father is the principal."

That's what she'd missed out on growing up in rodeo. The sense of community and the feeling of belonging in one place. And now she was going to have it in Bronco. In fact, she'd begun experiencing it with this gathering as Jack's friends welcomed her into the fold.

"What's that?" Jack asked, pointing to a piece of paper on the floor.

She shrugged.

"I'd better get it before someone slips on it." He crossed the room and picked it up. He was frowning when he returned to her side.

"What's it say?"

"It's another Bobby Stone flyer. It says '*a stone you'll never forget.*'"

"Isn't he the guy who died in that hiking accident that you told me about?"

"Yes. This is all too weird. He's been dead for three years. I don't understand why someone is bringing this up now after all this time."

She smoothed the lines from his forehead.

"Well, don't worry about it now. Let's go join everyone and enjoy this party. I want to show off my ring some more."

"So you like it?"

Audrey looked at the two-carat diamond solitaire set in a platinum band on her left hand. "I love it. Almost as much as I love you."

He kissed her. "That's what I want to hear."

Taking her hand, they passed a man seated at a bar, a stack of papers beside him. They were so involved with each other that they didn't notice him, or the way he focused on the flyer in Jack's hand. He took a sip of his drink and thought to himself, *If nothing else, I know that Bobby is on people's minds now. It's not enough. But it's a start.*

* * * * *